Meant For YOU

**A Sexy Flirty Dirty
Standalone Romance**

By Lili Valente

Meant For YOU

By Lili Valente

Self Taught Ninja Press

About the Book

What if there was one man—one gorgeous, brilliant, sexy as hell man—who was meant for you?

Yeah, well, there isn't. Love is a hard slog up a snowy mountain infested with rabid cougars, and meant-to-be love is just a lie. I learned that the hard way when all my romantic dreams went up in smoke, and the boy I loved walked away without looking back.

Or so I thought…

***

Seven years ago Fate ripped me away from the only girl I've ever loved. Now Addie and I are snowed in at a romantic mountain lodge, drinking cocoa around the Valentine's Day tree, and there's no way I'm going to let her slip away from me again.

One way or another, I'll prove to Adeline that we belong together.

She might not believe in love, but I do, and I'm going to use every sexy, wicked weapon at my disposal to convince my girl we're meant to be.

The best part of trying to win the one who got away? I know exactly what makes her laugh, what makes her melt, and what makes her squirm…

MEANT FOR YOU is a sexy, swoony, true love conquers all Standalone romantic comedy.

Dedicated to my family,
who make me feel like I'm exactly where
I'm meant to be.
Love always.

Part
ONE

~≈~ *And then there was you...* ~≈~

Chapter ONE

Seven Years Ago

Nate

As any self-respecting Pennsylvanian will tell you, there's a good chance the devil lives in New Jersey. The sulfuric turnpike smell, toxic waste dumps, abundance of creepy urban legends, and the New Jersians' rabid consumption of pork rolls and gravy-drenched French fries all point to some sort of demonic influence.

So when the hardware store where I worked went out of business the day after graduation, and I found myself with three months of unexpected freedom stretching out in front of me before it was time to leave for Duke, a road trip to investigate the New Jersey devil situation shot to the top of my to-do list. I'd just read a horror novel about a hellmouth located in Passaic

County and thought it would be interesting to see if the real life setting—a series of underground tunnels and storm drains near Clifton—did the book justice.

I'd spent most of my high school career playing football or running drills with the private coach my dad hired to help me get better at playing football—the *best* at playing football—but much to my old man's eternal frustration I preferred to spend my downtime reading instead of watching game tape in the basement. In books, there were no limits, no rules—at least not for writers brave enough to break them—and I couldn't conceive of something more exciting than a job with no rules.

I was eighteen. Rules—and my father, most of the time—were the enemy.

As I hiked down the culvert to the entrance to the Jersey hellmouth, picking my way around the rusted out shells of old cars, shattered beer bottles, soggy cardboard boxes, a few headless dolls, and other assorted detritus one would expect to find near a portal to a creepier dimension, I pondered rules and which ones I would have broken if I were the author of *The Devil You Need*.

I'm rewriting the ending to give a couple of secondary characters a happy ending, just to mess with the "almost everyone dies and then there's a terrible twist that assures you everyone who lived is totally fucked" horror novel convention, when

I turn a corner and find myself no longer alone.

There, standing under the "Entrance to Hellmouth Here →" sign helpfully spray painted on the concrete wall of the culvert, stands a pretty kid in overalls with dark brown curls, a heart-shaped face, and big blue eyes framed by a pair of wire-rimmed glasses. I meet her gaze across the trash-littered landscape, where someone thought it would be funny to dress a department store mannequin as a werewolf clown and leave it propped up against a shopping cart, and I laugh. I can't help it.

She smiles, cocking her head as she leans on her walking stick. "What's so funny?"

"Nothing. Sorry." I motion her way. "You're just not what I expected the devil to look like."

Her smile widens. "Interesting. You're *exactly* what I expected him to look like."

"Oh, yeah?" I ask, intrigued. "How so?"

"Well, the devil's supposed to be pretty, right?" She gives me an up and down look that's unnerving coming from a kid. "Tall, dark, and handsome with a smile that makes you think it's okay to stay and chat a while. And then before you know it you're dancing in the pale moonlight and your soul is just another charm on his necklace."

My smile fades. "Do your parents know you're out here by yourself?"

"Um, no. But my parents are pathologically overprotective, and I'm starting at Rutgers next fall. I figured it was time to start living my life on my own terms." She props a hand on her hip, which is curvier than I expect it to be beneath those overalls, and lifts her chin. "What about you, does your mommy know you're out exploring the hellmouth and talking to strangers?"

"No. She doesn't." I tip my head in acknowledgment of her well-executed dig. "But I'm headed to Duke next year, so I guess you and I are on the same page. What brings you to the hellmouth?"

"A book I read."

"*The Devil You Need?*"

"Yeah," she says with a grin. "You, too?"

"I have a thing for eighties horror. How about you?"

"Oh, I have a thing for everything. I like to push my reading boundaries, explore it all." She shrugs as she lifts a small boot, rolling her ankle. "The most beautiful thing we can experience is the mysterious, right?"

I blink, surprised again. "Einstein?"

Her eyes glitter as she laughs. "The pretty devil knows his quotes."

"I have no special talents," I quote, deciding I like this girl, and that I don't mind being called a pretty devil, either. "I am only passionately curious."

"I like that one, too." Her lips purse as she nods thoughtfully. "All right, then. Shall we go in together? A hellmouth seems like something that's more fun as a shared experience, don't you think?"

"I do. I'm Nate." I amble closer, holding out my hand.

"Adeline." She takes it, sending a shiver of electricity prickling across my skin.

It's not attraction, not exactly, not that first morning. It's a spark, a flicker of recognition, a warning that things are about to change in ways I never could have imagined when I woke up in my bed that morning, so certain the path was mapped and the way was clear.

***

But by the next time we meet up—on an allegedly haunted stretch of beach, to which Addie has brought a ghost-themed picnic and worn a vintage nineteen fifties bathing suit that makes it clear she's not a little girl, not even a little bit—I'm thinking about kissing her. I think about it all the way up and down the beach, through our picnic, into the water and back out again, the need to taste her clawing away at me as I wrap a towel around her shivering body.

"Thanks," she says, her teeth chattering. "Geez, that was cold. I can't feel my legs from the knees down."

I sit down next to her on the blanket, tugging my own towel around my shoulders. "But worth it, right? I never pass up a chance to get in the water."

"I'm not sure I believe you." Her tongue slips out, sweeping away the water beaded on her lips.

My brows lift. "Oh yeah? Why not?"

"I think you're hesitant to take certain plunges." She gazes up at me through her thick lashes with a smile that makes me want to push her back onto the blanket and kiss her until neither of us can breathe. "So what's it going to be, pretty devil? Are you going to kiss me, or what?"

I lean in, pressing my lips to hers, laying claim to her smart little mouth. And from that first brush of skin against skin, it's clear that this is something different than any kiss I've ever known. I get hard—instantly, urgently hard—but that isn't the strange part. Other girls have made me *want*, but Addie is the first to make me *ache*. The need to explore every inch of her—body, mind, and soul—swells in my chest as we kiss, making the moment when I finally roll her beneath me almost painfully sweet.

"You feel so good," I murmur against her lips, pulse spiking as she spreads her legs and I settle between them, rocking gently against her through our damp clothes.

"Wow," she says, breath coming faster. "*That* feels good."

My jaw clenches as my cock swells thicker, harder. "Want me to make it feel even better?" I tease my fingertips along the elastic at the top of her thigh, dying to slip my hand beneath her suit and find out if she's wet. "Best part about a haunted beach: there's no one around to see what we do on our blanket."

"That's true," she says, swallowing as my lips trail down her throat. "But, Nate?" She tugs lightly at my hair.

I pull back. "Yes, Adeline?"

"I'm only sixteen," she says, uncertainty in her eyes for the first time since we met. "I graduated early."

I brush the curls from her face. "So you really are Einstein."

"No, I'm just a nerd who was homeschooled and is good at taking tests." She rolls her eyes. "But I'm still living with my parents and will be for the foreseeable future, and I'm, um…not really allowed to date. I thought you should know."

I nod, but it's hard to think straight when her thighs are wrapped around me. "Does that mean you want me to stop?"

"I don't know." Her teeth dig into her bottom lip. "To be honest, I'm not sure where we're going. I mean, I *know*, but I don't *know*. If you know what I mean?"

"You've never been with someone," I say, putting the pieces together. I might not be as smart as she is, but I'm pretty quick on my feet.

And I'm usually quick to run from virgins as fast as those feet will carry me—being someone's first time is the kind of thing that has always seemed more scary than sexy—but I don't pull away.

I stay, watching her cheeks flush as she confesses, "I've never even kissed someone. At least not if you don't count Gary Yates behind the equipment shed at church camp last year, and I don't because you've made it clear to me that Gary had no flipping idea what he was doing."

I smile, not bothering to keep the smug from my expression.

She laughs, slapping me lightly on the shoulder. "Oh, stop. I was just thinking how nice it is that you're not an arrogant jerk even though you're stupidly beautiful."

"There's nothing wrong in taking pride in things you do well, Adeline." I press a kiss to her cheek and then to her neck, loving the way she shivers as I murmur into her ear, "And if you want me to show you all the ways I can make you feel good, I would love to." I force myself to pull my hand away from the curve of her hip, wanting to be sure we're on the same page before this goes any further. "But I'm only here until the end of August. I'm taking sixteen credits and every spare second I'm not in class is going to be eaten up by football. I'm not going to have time to make a long distance relationship work, not even with someone like you."

Her eyes narrow. "Someone like me?"

"Someone smart and beautiful and totally…weird," I finish, though that isn't exactly what I mean. I don't mean weird, I mean different, special, but Addie doesn't seem upset.

"I think you're smart and weird, too," she says, wrapping her arms around my neck. "And more exciting than reading a book."

"That's high praise."

Her gaze drops to my lips. "I know. Don't make me regret it, summer boy."

"I won't, summer girl," I promise, as I cover her mouth with mine. I kiss her until she's squirming beneath me, silently begging for more, and then slowly, carefully, I give it to her. I brush my thumbs across her nipples through her suit while she makes these hot, sexy sounds at the back of her throat that drive me wild.

Finally, I can't resist tugging the fabric down low enough to get my mouth on her bare skin and suck her nipple between my lips. I tease her with my tongue, laving her swollen flesh until she moans, digs her hands into my bare shoulders, and murmurs, "Please, oh please, Nate." Only then do I slide her swimsuit to one side and slip my fingers between her legs.

That first moment, when I realize how hot and wet she is, almost destroys me. Imagination can be a dangerous thing, and as Addie lifts into my hand, crying out my name, mine starts working overtime. Just imagining how incredible it would feel to push inside her, to make her come on my cock, is almost enough to make me go.

Which would probably be for the best. I don't

have a condom and making out under a towel and having full-on sex on the beach are two entirely different things. If someone happened by right now, I could have Addie covered in a second. But if I were in the middle of something more serious, I'm not sure I could stop.

God, I don't want to stop.

I want to go and go. I want to make her come on my fingers and then strip off her clothes and show her how much better it is when we're climbing together, every stroke of my hips taking us both closer to the edge.

"Oh my God." She trembles as I find her clit and rub it in gentle circles. "Oh my God, Nate."

"Have you come before?" I continue to slide my fingers in and out of where she's so wet that I'm dying to taste her. But not this time, not yet. I don't want to go too far, too fast. I don't want to scare her away. I want every minute of the summer she's promised.

"Yes, but—" Her words cut off in a moan. "Oh, God. But not like this, not like—" Her back arches, her lips part, and her delicate features twist. I know she's coming even before I feel her body tighten around my fingers.

"Fuck, yes, Addie." I rock my throbbing length against her thigh as she rides the wave, the look on her face the sexiest thing I've ever seen. I groan, eyes squeezing shut as I come so hard, insanely hard, simply from the friction of rubbing against her through our clothes.

I should be ashamed of myself for having the self-control of a fourteen-year-old, but when I see Addie's blissed out expression, all I can do is smile. "Good?"

"Let's do that all the time," she says, grinning. "Every day until you leave."

***

We sneak away so often that Addie has to invent a fake volunteer job and I start lying to my dad, saying I'm meeting friends in Jersey to scrimmage so he won't ride my ass about getting out of shape before training starts in the fall.

I'm not getting out of shape; I'm logging more miles on the trail than I have in years. Adeline and I hike to every haunted corner of New Jersey and then move into Pennsylvania, joining a rock-climbing expedition to an ancient burial ground hosted by a group of paranormal investigators that Addie assures me her über-Catholic mother would say are going straight to hell.

She giggles as she adds that what I'm doing to her under our shared sleeping bag is also probably grounds for eternal damnation, or at least a good long stint in purgatory. But that doesn't stop me from making her come on my mouth so hard I have to cover her lips with my hand to keep the sounds she makes from being overheard by the people in the next tent.

And when she whispers that she's ready, that she wants me, I don't hesitate to roll on a condom and push inside her for the first time.

There is no guilt, no hesitation, nothing but bliss and pleasure because that's how it is with Addie. It feels like I've known her forever, and been in love with her even longer.

Maybe it's the magic of summer or the crazy way we met or the fact that she's shown me what making love is supposed to feel like—close and beautiful and so perfect it's almost scary—but I don't question the certainty that this isn't the first time I've fallen for Adeline.

And by the end of the summer, as the August nights grow cooler and the first leaves turn golden at the edges, I don't question the voice in my head that says all my plans aren't worth a single precious hair on her head.

Addie has taught me what it's like to be in love, real love, the kind that sinks its claws in deep and invites your big plans to go fuck themselves because plans are a dime a dozen and love is hitting a target the size of a pinprick in the dark.

The big plans aren't mine, anyway. My father is the one who wants me to major in pre-law while playing football for his alma mater. I went along with pre-law because I knew he would throw a fit if I applied to the creative writing program, and football because I'm good at it and it seemed stupid to stop doing something I'm good at just because it stopped being fun years ago.

But this summer with Addie has been a wake up call, a reminder that life is incredible and magical, just like making love to her.

I don't want to settle for good enough, or making my father happy. I want the big adventure. I want to explore and dig deep and wring every drop of excitement and mystery out of the world, and I want to do it with this beautiful, brilliant person by my side.

***

"Getting nervous yet?" I ask as I turn off onto a gravel road that isn't much more than a drainage ditch, heading deep into the mountains near New Paltz.

"Do I look nervous?" Addie props her bare feet on the dashboard. "Seriously, Nate, if my mom hasn't called to check up on my 'charity work' yet, I don't see why she would start this weekend."

"Because we're going to be gone for two nights instead of one," I say, willing to play devil's advocate while we still have time to turn around and get back to Addie's house before nightfall. "And because you've been fighting with her about living on campus."

Addie's lips twist. "I have a full scholarship that includes room and board. It's stupid for me to stay at home when I could live next door to the library and be able to walk to my classes in ten minutes."

"And be able to sneak your boyfriend in to sleep over every night," I say, deciding now is as good a time as any to tell her I can't quit her and hope she can't quit me, either.

She goes still, her gaze fixed on the road ahead, but she doesn't say a word, not a word, for so long that I can't help asking, "Did you hear me, Einstein?"

"I heard you. Pull over." She waits until I pull to the side of the narrow road and shove the car into park before she turns to face me, pushing her glasses higher on her nose. "Did you just say what I think you just said?"

"That I want to sleep with you every night? Assuming you're lucky enough to land a private room or your roommate isn't a bitch about overnight guests?"

"And how are you going to manage that? It's a seven hour drive from Duke to Rutgers." Her frown deepens. "And you're the one who said this is only for the summer."

"I may have made a miscalculation," I say softly.

"About how far it is between schools?"

"About how much I was going to love you." I reach out, taking her hand as tears fill her eyes. "I'm sorry, Ad. If you need to take time to think about what you want, I understand, but I've already made my decision. I'm transferring to Rutgers and joining the Writers House program. I'm going to learn how to write better stories and keep loving you because those are the things that make me feel alive, and I don't want to go back to doing what other people think is best for me. I can't. Not after this summer, and you, and everything we—"

"Oh, shut up." She blinks, sending a tear down her cheek.

Before I can apologize again, or find a better way to say all the things I'm feeling, she says, "Of course I want you to keep loving me. I just wish you'd said something sooner so I wouldn't have spent the last week crying myself to sleep because you were leaving next Friday." She sniffs. "I've been flipping miserable, but I promised I was okay with the summer so I tried to act like I was okay. But I wasn't, P.D. Not even a little bit."

P.D., short for pretty devil. The nickname has become another shared joke, but today is the first time that I've actually felt like a devil. A stupid devil.

"Fuck, I'm an asshole. I'm sorry, Einstein." Relief rushes through me as she dives into my arms, hugging me tight. I bend over her, kissing her wild hair. "I'll make it up to you, I promise."

"Yes," she says, voice muffled against my chest. "You will. I want pancakes in bed tomorrow. And then I want you to lick the syrup off my fingers."

"Is that the only place I get to lick syrup from?" My hand moves to cup her ass through her faded jeans.

"You can do whatever you want with the syrup." She pulls back, meeting my naughty look with a prim one so cute I have no choice but to kiss the tip of her nose. "As long as we do it in your sleeping bag so I don't end up with ants in mine."

"Done," I say, already imagining how hot it's going to be to lick maple syrup from her nipples and the hollow beside her hipbone and the sweet folds between her legs.

***

I do such a dangerous job of imagining it, in fact, that by the time we get to the deserted campground—apparently other paranormal enthusiasts aren't free to go camping on a Tuesday night—I'm so hard I can't wait to set up the tent. I pull Adeline into the backseat and get her out of her jeans as fast as humanly possible, while she kisses me like I'm oxygen, water, adventure, and all life's other necessities rolled up together.

It's so hot that I end up ripping the buttons on her shirt in my hurry to get her tits in my mouth. I suck and bite and make love to her nipples until she's panting my name. And then she straddles me and I'm suddenly inside her, buried deep, and it's perfect, so insanely fucking good to feel her breath comes hot and fast on my lips as she rides me, grinding so deep that my cock hits the end of her with every thrust.

I'm so gone, so wild, that all it takes is her voice rough in my ear, saying, "I'm coming, Nate, I'm coming!" to send me over.

I dig my fingers into the swells of her ass and

come so hard, so long, so fierce and fantastic that it's almost more than my body can take. I go out of my head for a second, out of my skin, out of space and time.

When I finally drift back, Addie is still straddling me, watching me with an intent expression on her face.

"Hey." I pat her bottom. "You okay?"

"I don't know. On the one hand, that was the hottest thing ever. But on the other hand…" She points a meaningful finger down to where I'm going soft inside her without a single thing to separate my hot, pulsing flesh from hers.

I curse. "Condom. How could we forget the condom?"

"Is that a serious question?" she asks, arching a brow.

I shake my head. Of course it isn't a serious question. I know exactly how we forgot the condom. We forgot it because the sex was explosive and crazy hot and we both went out of our heads for a little while.

"Okay." I swallow as I run a soothing hand up and down her bare back. "We'll get dressed, head back into New Palz, and find a pharmacy where they sell the morning-after pill."

"Except that I'll need a prescription for it because I'm under seventeen," Addie says, making me curse again. She smiles in response, which confuses me until she adds, "So it's a good thing I had my friend Steph get one for me a few weeks ago before she left for Princeton. I've got it in my purse."

My head falls back against the seat as I go limp with relief. "Thank God. You scared me. *We* scared me. That can't happen again."

"Agreed." She leans in, pressing a soft kiss to my lips. "As soon as school starts, I'll go to the campus health center and get on the pill. Then we won't have to worry."

"You're very smart." I pull her in for a deeper kiss, humming into her mouth as her tongue slips out to tease mine. "Though, I admit, I do like getting out of control with you."

"Me, too," she says, pulsing her hips. "And I like you with nothing in between. I love feeling your skin against mine."

I grip her ass, pulling her closer as I start to get thicker. "Should we get a condom before I make you come again, beautiful?"

"Doesn't seem like it matters now." She laughs softly at my no doubt unabashedly thrilled expression. "I say we make the most of our day of freedom, baby."

"I couldn't agree more." I roll her beneath me, and this time I set the pace. I slide my hand beneath her, tilting her pelvis as I thrust inside her until her sharp gasp lets me know I've found the spot that makes her wild. I fuck her harder than I ever have, driving in fast and deep until she comes screaming my name, holding nothing back.

And when we're done, I'm high, dizzy, drunk

on the knowledge that she's mine and the future is ours and that soon I'll get to have her bare every time.

I'm so out of my head that I don't think twice when she suggests a hike before we set up camp. Yes, it's late afternoon, and the sun sets earlier between the mountains, but it's still summer and the sun is shining and I'm so full of energy that the thought of being patient with my piece of shit tent isn't appealing.

***

We strap on our CamelBaks, spray each other with bug spray to keep off the ticks, and head into the woods. For the first couple of hours, we're so busy talking books and school and plans that we don't pay much attention to where we're going. According to the map, the Harmony Ridge trail is pretty basic—a big circle that leads up to the top of the ridge and then dips back into the valley before rolling back up to the campground again.

The campground was once the site of a leper colony in the late eighteen hundreds. The foundations of the old buildings are still visible if you take the shorter Lost Souls trail down toward the river, but Addie and I agreed that we would save exploring that until the morning. We've yet to find any evidence of paranormal activity in any of our adventures, but that doesn't mean we aren't spooked by creepy places, especially after dark. We agree that weirdness is best investigated early in the morning, and we're usually headed for home no later than four or five o'clock. Addie's mom's rules against boys and riding in cars and any combination of the two means that most of our dates have taken place during the daylight hours.

This will only be the fourth time we've spent the night together. Thoughts of making love to Addie again after dinner, taking advantage of the pill she's brought one more time before it's back to condoms is enough to keep me distracted for a good thirty minutes after I should have realized something was wrong.

But my head isn't where it should be, and it's Addie who eventually realizes we must have gotten off the trail.

"Look at where the sun's setting." She points to the ridge on the other side of the valley. "It shouldn't be that far away. We must have missed the switchback somewhere and veered onto another trail."

"Shit, you're right. Let me check the app." But when I try to access the trailblazer app, my phone can't connect. Thankfully, Addie has the paper map in her pack. We get it out and spread it open on a tree stump with a killer view of the forest below, but none of the spur trails shown would have led us in this particular direction.

"Weird," Addie says, chewing on the pad of her thumb. "So what do you think? It will be getting dark soon. Do we retrace our steps or

head through the woods down to the river and—
"

"And then follow the river back to camp," I finish, squinting at the rapidly disappearing sun.

"We've got bug spray so we shouldn't get too covered in bites," she says. "Though the poison ivy is pretty gnarly."

"But there's a path through it." I point to the bare forest floor under the thicker growing trees. "And we're wearing jeans. I think we should take our chance with the poison ivy. We'll get back to camp twice as fast and won't end up wandering around in the woods after dark without a flashlight."

"I should have brought the flashlight. I wasn't thinking."

"No, I should have brought it." I put my arm around her, kissing her forehead. "You already did your part to prove you're super prepared."

She hums in agreement. "I did, didn't I?"

I tuck the map into my back pocket with a smile. "Let's do this."

***

Forty-five minutes later, we still haven't reached the bottom of the valley or the river or another trail leading back toward the campground and the sun is shining through the trees at a sharp slant that promises it'll be gone any second.

I'm silently starting to freak out, wondering what I'm going to do if Addie and I are still out here when it gets dark, when the ground dips sharply and I stumble. Addie grabs onto my arm, and we both go skidding through the loose leaves, coming to a stop at the edge of a clearing.

And there, in the middle of the woods is a tiny cabin with smoke coming out of the chimney and one hell of a fight going on inside. I can't make out what the people are saying, but it sounds like a man and a woman, and they're clearly in the middle of World War Three.

I'm about to suggest we get the hell out of here—screw asking for directions from people who sound like they're about to kill each other—when someone inside starts screaming. It's a weird, distorted sound, almost like it's coming through a radio, but it's the same woman who was shouting a moment before.

Only now she sounds like she's being carved into tiny pieces while the man roars something about her being a whore.

"We have to do something," Addie hisses, gripping my arm tight. "Nate, we have to do something!"

"But what?" I ask. "I can't call 911. I'm not getting reception."

Addie glances around, bending down fast and scooping up a rock about the size of a baseball. "Do it, please," she says, pointing to the window. "We have to do something, and you can throw harder than I can."

Inside, the woman screams again, and I move without thinking, hurling the rock at the window with all the strength in my star quarterback arm. The second the glass shatters, I snatch Addie's hand and haul ass down the hill.

We're almost out of sight, when someone in the house cries out something that sounds a lot like—

"Addie!"

—and Adeline spins to look back, her eyes wide in her pale face.

But I don't let her stop. I wrap my arm around her waist and haul her bodily down the mountain, refusing to let her be shot by angry hillbillies who consider breaking a window a shooting offense. I carry her until she starts sprinting beside me, both of us setting new personal speed records as we crash through the trees.

We keep going, pushing hard until the river comes into sight. Only then, when we're minutes from the safety of the car, do we pause to catch our breath.

"You heard it, right?" Addie braces her hands on her knees, sucking in air. "You heard someone call out my name?"

"Could have been Abby, too, or…" I shake my head. "I don't know, some other name that sounds like yours."

"Like what?" She paces back and forth, her troubled gaze fixed on the mountain as her breath slowly returns to normal. "Not many names sound like mine, and the voice was almost familiar, wasn't it?"

"I don't know. Honestly, my heart was pounding so hard by that point I wasn't paying attention to anything except getting out of there."

Her brow knits. "Do you think she's okay? Do you think he…?" She trails off without finishing the sentence, but I know what she's thinking.

"No, I don't think so. I think we scared them, and they stopped fighting."

"I hope so." She turns to me with a sigh. "But it was so weird, Nate. When I looked back, it was so dark inside the house. Dark like the bottom of a pit in the middle of the night. I couldn't see anything, but I swear I could feel someone looking at me. Right at me." She shudders. "I think I finally get that saying about someone walking over your grave."

"No one walked over your grave." I take her hand, tugging her back into motion along the path beside the riverbank. "And no one's going to. How about we forget camping and go get a room in New Paltz? I've got enough to pay for a night and then we can find somewhere sane to camp tomorrow."

She nods, picking up her pace beside me. "Yes, yes, and yes. That's the smartest idea you've had since you begged me to be you girlfriend for real."

I smile. "I didn't really beg. But I would have."

She glances my way, her eyes flashing in the setting sun. "I know."

***

We make it back to the car and out of the forest without any more drama, and by the time we've checked into a hotel, grabbed a pizza from the mom-and-pop place down the street, and settled in to watch television while we devour an extra large pie, we've put the memory of our close call with the woods and the hillbillies behind us. We don't even consider calling the police. Addie's sixteen, I threw a rock through someone's window, and those people *chose* to live out in the middle of nowhere together.

Maybe they did that so they could have the freedom to scream at each other whenever they want without other people sticking their noses in. In any case, it seems best to forget about the weird and enjoy the rest of our trip.

The next day we get up early, head to the lake, and swim until we're too exhausted to do anything but lay like snakes, basking in the sun. Addie falls asleep, and soon I do, too. When I wake up, the beach is deserted and Addie has slipped off her top and is lying next to me with a wickedly cute, slightly nervous look on her face. She's so fucking sexy I can't resist grabbing my phone and snapping a picture.

At first, she insists I delete it, but then I show her the shot, and how beautiful she is, and she lets me pull out my real camera and take a few more. She's so magical, so breathtaking and sexy, just like the first time I kissed her on the beach, except now she has tan lines because we've had the most amazing first summer together.

But it won't be the last.

"Next summer, we'll go to the Grand Canyon." I kiss her, cupping her breast in my hand. "You and me, epic road trip."

"I won't be eighteen yet." She bites her lip as I tease her nipple between my fingers. "And I can't keep lying to my parents. I want you to meet them."

"You think that's a good idea?"

"It's a great idea. You're wonderful, and they'll love you—as long as they don't think we're having premarital sex."

"That may be a problem." I slip my hand down the front of her bikini bottoms, finding her clit. "Because I'm pretty sure it's written all over my face how much I love fucking you, Einstein."

She smiles as she arches into my touch. "It is. It's one of the things I love best about you, P.D."

"I love you, too," I murmur into the soft skin at her neck as I rub her clit in firm circles. "I love you so much, Addie."

"Me, too." She tugs at the top of my swim trunks. "Now. Please."

"What if someone shows up?" I ask, but I'm already reaching for a condom.

"Everyone's gone except us." She lifts her hips, letting me pull her bottoms down her legs. "And I need you. So much."

I slide the condom on and then I slide inside Adeline, making love to her on the beach in broad daylight, but no one sees her come but me. No one hears her call my name like I'm all she needs in the whole world. It's like the universe was made for the two of us and nothing else dares to intrude when we're together.

Everything is…perfect.

My guard is so fucking down it's like I never had one to begin with. Like I never had the sense to worry about all the shit that could, and so often does, go wrong.

***

The next morning, I drop Addie at the end of her street to walk home—and pretend that she's spent the past two nights chaperoning at a church camp—and head for the highway. I'm pulling onto the 895 when my phone rings. It's my dad, telling me to get my ass home, do not pass go, do not pretend to be practicing football in New Jersey like a "lying little bastard," do not collect a single damn dollar because he's emptied out my checking account.

I know the game is up, but I have no clue how bad it's going to be.

I've been so drunk on Addie and high on love that I've forgotten how much my father hates to lose.

***

It isn't until a month later, as I'm standing outside my English 101 class, the only course in my entire damned schedule that I look forward to, that I realize it isn't worth it.

Survival isn't worth it.

I don't want to survive, I want to *live*, and I want to do it with Addie, even if we only have a few days together before it all falls apart.

An hour later, everything I own is shoved in my trunk and I'm headed north, bound for Adeline. But when I get to her house, she's gone. Vanished without a trace, at least not one her irate mother is willing to share with me.

I spend the next three days tracking down Addie's friends and her piano teacher and her math tutor, but no one knows where she's gone. The trail is cold, and by the time I've slept in my car for three nights, so am I.

I hate myself for what's happened, and for leaving Addie the way I did, but it's time to make a plan, and to get the hell out of the country in case Dad decides to make good on his threats. My grandmother buys me a ticket to London, where my cousin lets me crash in his spare room while I apply to creative writing programs. I get accepted for the winter term in Manchester, find a job, and spend the next few years making sure I'm so busy I don't have time to think about the things—or the people—I've left behind.

Eventually I land my first big article, my second, my third, and then, by the grace of the journalistic gods, my piece on social media detox is picked up by *Time* magazine.

Suddenly, I've got a genuine career on my hands and even less time to think.

***

The years go by, one adventure spiraling into another, and I feel like I'm awake, alive, living the dream. But I might as well be in a fucking coma. At least as far as my heart is concerned.

No matter how many girls I date, how many women I sleep with, how often I try to get past the fifth week of a relationship and into the sixth, it never works. Because none of those women are the girl with the wire glasses and crooked smile, who made me feel like summer would never end.

None of them are Adeline, the person I was once so fucking sure was meant for me.

LILI VALENTE

Part
TWO

᨞᨞᨞ *You again...* ᨞᨞᨞

Present Day

From the text archives of Adeline "Addie" Klein
and Shane Willoughby Falcone

Adeline: Shane? Are you awake?

Shane: Of course, it's five a.m.

Adeline: Oh crap, it is! I'm sorry!
Forget I texted. Go back to sleep.
you're getting very sleepy

Shane: I am not! LOL! I wasn't sleeping, I
promise.

Adeline: Sometimes it's hard to tell if someone is
being sarcastic via text…

Shane: I'm never sarcastic about getting up early. Four a.m. to seven a.m. are the best hours of the day. I've already done yoga, fed the orchids, booked a pregnancy massage, organized the recycling, and contemplated the effect of climate change on coastal property in Southeast Asia.

Adeline: You're moving to Southeast Asia?!

Shane: No. I've just been reading too many Discovery magazine articles about coastal erosion, mutating viruses, and the dangers inherent in making DNA editing something any kid with a CRISPR can do in his home lab. Turns out, the world is a lot scarier once you've committed to bringing an innocent life into it. So it's good that you texted to take my mind off of my troubles ☺.
What's up?

Adeline: Nothing really. It's not a big deal. Let's talk about you!
How are you feeling? Still having afternoon sickness?

Shane: Don't you dare, Adeline! Tell me what's flipping around in your squirrel brain. What has you up and fretting at five a.m.?

Adeline: But you already sound stressed…

Shane: I am not stressed, but I will be if you don't spill the goods.
Don't make me come down there and knock on the door while Miss Eloise is still in her pajamas.

Adeline: God, no! She'll skin me alive for having someone over without asking!

Shane: Then someone better start typing…
Tick, tick, tick…
walks to the door
contemplates bringing some of those prunes Miss Eloise likes so that she can serenade you later when they start to take effect

Adeline: Jesus, anything but the prunes! I'll talk! I'll talk!

Shane: I'm listening…

Adeline: *heavy sigh*
I didn't want to bother you while you and Jake were on your honeymoon, but it occurred to me a few days ago that I hadn't asked you not to mention me to the man we saw in the park with Aidan. You, know, the one's who training to work for Magnificent Bastard Consulting? Nate?

Shane: You mean Nate of the killer cheekbones, whiskey and honey voice, and sinfully broad shoulders, who you had wild and crazy sexy times with all summer long before he went away to college. That Nate?

Adeline: Um. Yes. That one.
Please tell me you haven't said anything to him about me living in the city…

Shane: Of course not. I've been too busy to make it to Bash and Penny's place for poker night, but I wouldn't have said anything anyway.
You clearly aren't a fan of Mr. Casey, Addie, and I'm not a fan of introducing unnecessary stress into a friend's life. Your secret is safe with me.

Adeline: Oh good. *melts into a relief-puddle*
Thank you so much!

Shane: You're welcome. Though I still say you should let me talk to Bash and get Nate fired. If he's got you this spooked, he's not the sort of person who's cut out for helping the unlucky in love get back at their evil exes.
Bash would be better off cutting him loose and looking for someone else to play the sexy businessman type.

Adeline: No, Nate will do a fine job. A great job, probably.
Like I said before, he's good at pretending to feel things he doesn't really feel.
And I don't want to mess up his life. I just have

no interest in seeing him again. I have better
things to do with my time. Like fetch Eloise more
gourmet laxatives or shine all the silver with a
cotton swab or watch light brown paint dry.

Shane: Light brown paint is the worst.
Why does the HOA insist on redoing the
hallways in cardboard box brown every few years,
Addie? It vexes me.

Adeline: Brown is the color of despair.

Shane: I agree, and for what it's worth…
Well, I know I only talked to Nate briefly, but I'm
still comfortable saying that you're too good for
him. You've got a one-in-a-million heart, Adeline
Klein. Anyone who would take that for granted is
a putz not worthy to lick your penny loafers.
Breaking up with you was the stupidest thing he's
ever done.

Adeline: Aw, well… Thank you.
It was a little more complicated than that,
but…thank you.

Shane: It's always complicated when it comes to
men we used to love, sweets.
But that doesn't mean you don't deserve
someone who will appreciate how very special
you are.

Adeline: I love you, but you have to stop before you make me cry.

Shane: Stopping right now.
Here, have an emoji rendition of *Let it Go*.
It makes everything better.

Adeline: LOL. Why do you have this on your phone?

Shane: The power went out at our cabin while Jake and I were on our honeymoon. Writing songs in emoji format helped pass the time when I got tired of Text Twist and Candy Crush.

Adeline: I would think you guys could have come up with more entertaining things to do in the dark...

Shane: Two people can only bang so much, Addie. Especially when one person has morning sickness and the other is recovering from surgery.

Adeline: Good point.

Shane: All right, I'm off to make tea and toast. Want to come up and share my marmalade?

Adeline: I have to get Eloise's bag packed for her doctor's appointment. But thanks for the talk.

Shane: We didn't talk. I promised NOT to talk.
But if you ever actually want to do a post mortem
on old Nate and give me lots of good reasons to
hate him, I'm here.

Adeline: Thank you. But I won't.
I put the Nate baggage away a long time ago.
Some things are better off six feet under.

Shane: Assuming they'll stay buried…

Adeline: I don't believe in zombies.

Shane: But you believe in vampires, right?
Since you live with one?

Adeline: Omg, you made me laugh out loud.
Loudly out loud. Now Eloise will want to know
what's so funny and you know I'm the worst liar.

Shane: Seriously though, Eloise being a vampire
really would explain a lot, wouldn't it? The
paleness, the aversion to sunlight and happiness,
the way her eyes get all feverish when she's
making someone squirm in misery.
Maybe she's one of those emotional vampires
who feed on misery…

Adeline: You have to stop!

Shane: At least we know she's not a succubus, you know the kind of vampires who—

Adeline: Oh God. Yes! I mean, no! Stop, my stomach is starting to hurt.

Shane: So you know what a succubus is?

Adeline: I know exactly what a succubus is. Thanks for making me picture Eloise naked.

Shane: Naked and getting biz-zay…

Adeline: You really do take things too far sometimes.

Shane: All part of my charm
Say hello to Eloise for me.

Adeline: I will, you wicked thing.

Shane: Well, you know what they say—
If you can't be good, be good at it. *devil emoji*
See you later, sweet Addie. And as always, your secrets are safe with me.

Chapter THREE

Adeline

I stare at the devil emoji on my screen for longer than I should, thinking about pretty devils and how naïve I used to be. Just a stupid kid pretending to be grown up for the summer.

I think about that girl a lot. Sixteen-year-old Addie with her smart mouth and big dreams, so sure of herself and the love of a boy who touched her like she was the only thing that mattered. Sometimes I hate her confidence and those happy memories of the past that float around inside me, making me aware of my not-so-happy present. Other times I want to reach back through time, give teen me a big hug, and thank her for giving me that beautiful summer.

One summer of being wild and loved and oh-so-brave before my pretty devil proved he wasn't so pretty after all, not in the ways that count, and left without even saying goodbye.

"Adeline!" Eloise screeches my name from somewhere deeper in the apartment and I jump to attention, quickly deleting my text conversation with Shane, just in case Eloise decides to "borrow" my phone again to paw through my personal messages.

"Coming!" I tuck the phone into my cleavage—one area I can be reasonably certain Eloise will leave unmolested—and hurry to tidy my room and get dressed, feeling strangely at odds with myself. But maybe it's not so strange, really. It's not just knowing Nate's in my city that's making me crazy. Eloise does her share to tighten the screws.

The pressure has been building for months, *years*, even.

On this morning in early February, with the city outside my twelfth-story window covered in white and the Central Park trees shaggy with fresh snow, I have been the faithful live-in companion to widow Eloise Rosewell-Du Pont for nearly seven years.

Seven years of getting up at five a.m. to fix her tea so that it could cool to the ideal temperature of 62.8 degrees and be ready in the sitting room when her maid, Mina, finishes helping her bathe and dress. Seven years of reading the New York Times aloud while Eloise bemoans every modern development since 1964. Seven years of wheeling her to her weekly PT appointments while she finds fault with my speed, no matter how fast or slow I roll her, and then sitting on the stoop outside the therapist's office because Eloise doesn't want anyone in the waiting room to mistake me for her granddaughter, Sylvia Elizabeth Louise Rosewell-Du Pont.

Sylvia, who is getting her doctorate in cellular biology, is engaged to the son of the banker who owns half the upper east side, is accomplished, poised, and attractive—different from me in every way, except for an unfortunate gene for curly hair that responds equally poorly to New York City humidity.

"That *hair*," Eloise is fond of saying, the thin skin around her mouth puckering as she surveys my dark mane of fuzz. "You really should wear a scarf, Adeline. In my day, women knew when to cover their heads. Not to mention the rest of themselves."

For years, I have worn nothing but long skirts, modest button-ups, and formless sweaters. I have a closet full of what my friend Shane calls "dour librarian casual," and still Eloise seems to think that I'm dressing to seduce the helpless men of New York City. The occasional catcalls from construction workers are due to the siren's song of my wide-leg, pleated khakis—"women in pants give men *ideas*, Adeline"—and Kevin, the homeless man who bows and mutters poetry every time I walk by his corner is doe-eyed because I've encouraged him with my feminine wiles.

And maybe I do encourage him. Just the tiniest bit.

It's nice to be told you're beautiful every once in a while, even by someone with only a handful of teeth and a smell like he's been sleeping in the same clothes since last Valentine's Day.

I should have looked for another position two years ago when Eloise broke her hip getting out of the bath and started insinuating the accident was my fault, even though *she* was the one who decided to get out of the tub without ringing for help. Or maybe a year ago, when she started sending me on increasingly wild scavenger hunts for obscure food items found only in the most dangerous and/or isolated corners of the city.

Satisfying my employer's cravings has become increasingly risky, and I've come to suspect that there's more motivating my missions than a hankering for lemon-misted prunes or black market caviar. Either Eloise craves the entertainment of my survival stories—I've spent two hours trapped in the cellar of a Chinatown fish monger, was frisked during a raid of a Jamaican fruit market, and ended up blindfolded in the meat-packing district, all for the sad carcass of an exotic French bird Eloise took two bites of and declared "too crunchy"—or the old bat is trying to kill me.

It's like Shane said one afternoon, right after I'd finished relating the tale of a harrowing search for an exotic Sardinian cheese:

"I try to give everyone the benefit of the doubt, Addie. But as I've gotten older, I've realized that some people actually enjoy poisoning the well."

I laugh, tossing my taco wrapper into a bin as we turn onto the path leading past the Central Park Zoo. "Well, thankfully, no one was poisoned. I didn't end up finding the Casu Marzu. And even if I had, I was going to strongly encourage Eloise to skip it. I read up on it on my way to the cheese monger. Apparently the maggots that are introduced to soften the cheese with their digestive enzymes are left inside *the wheel when it's shipped out for sale. They're still alive when it's served and can jump up to six inches when disturbed by a fork or spoon."*

"Oh my." Shane lays a hand over her baby bump. "Thank God I'm out of the first trimester or you would be seeing my tacos right now. That's the most revolting thing I've ever heard, Adeline."

I wince. "Sorry. I forgot about your delicate condition."

"Oh, pish, I'm not delicate." Shane wrinkles her nose. "Far from it. I'm tough as nails. That's why poison people leave me alone. They take one look in my eyes and realize there's no point in trying to bring me down. I may look soft, but under the fluffy hair and pink nail polish I'm forged of titanium."

She hooks her arm through mine as we meander deeper into the park, giving my bicep a light squeeze. "But I worry about you, sweets. I hope you won't take this the wrong way, but I think you're made of softer stuff. Soft, wonderful stuff that is precious in a hard world, but...." She sighs. "Well, I would just hate to see a well-poisoner like Eloise get to your groundwater and take your sparkle away."

My throat goes tight, and the back of my nose stings in a way I can't blame on the late autumn wind. "Oh, she's not that bad. She doesn't mean to be difficult. It's just the way she is."

And I wasn't always so soft. *I used to be strong, but that was a long time ago, before I learned that forgiveness and forever weren't in my future, and that love can't be trusted.*

"The way she is with you, *love," Shane corrects gently.* "I've never heard her talk to anyone else the way she grouches at you. She takes advantage of the fact that you're dependent on her for work and housing and everything else. And the past few months..." *She shakes her head.* "I don't know. It almost seems like she's been playing with you, doesn't it? Seeing how far she can push you before you push back."

I huddle deeper into my coat. "Well, she's going to be waiting a good long while, if that's the case. I can't push back. She's my boss and my only work reference. I was seventeen when I came to live with her, Shane. I've never had another job. I'm not qualified to do anything else but indulge Eloise." *I shrug.* "And besides, I owe her. A lot. Back then I had no money and nowhere else to go. Without Eloise I have no idea how I would have survived."

"I totally get it, babes. But things are different now." *Shane pulls me to the side of the path and turns to face me with a big smile.* "I've already talked to Jake, and we both agree that you need out of that penthouse of horrors. We *adore you so much and want to help, so we thought we could put down the money for you to get your own place!"*

I blink dumbly, while the rest of my features go slack with disbelief. Surely, she must be joking.

"We'll co-sign the lease if you need us to," Shane prattles on, "and cover your first six months of rent and living expenses. That way you'll have plenty of time to find another job and save for your rainy-day fund." She waves a gloved hand. "And we honestly don't care if you ever pay us back, but if your pride won't let you accept a gift, then the debt will be interest free and you can take as long as you need to settle up."

I swallow hard, gratitude and shame wrestling in my chest, making me feel vaguely nauseous. "Oh, no, I couldn't, Shane. I really couldn't. I couldn't take advantage of our friendship like that."

"You wouldn't be taking advantage! I have plenty of money, and there is nothing I enjoy more than investing in people I believe in." She takes my hand, her grip strong inside her fluffy pink mitten. "And I believe in you, Adeline Klein. You are clever and sweet and a wonderful friend, and I think you deserve to be happy."

"I am happy." It isn't a lie, at least not completely. I'm not happy, but I'm not miserable, either. Most of the time I'm pleasantly…neutral.

And I owe that to Eloise.

Eloise took me in when no one else would. She gave me a job and a room to call my own and never asked any uncomfortable questions.

In the beginning, I had assumed she avoided awkward subjects because she knew my parents had disowned me.

Later, I realized that she simply had no interest in the personal lives of "the help." But that was okay, too.

I appreciate the anonymity of being Eloise's companion, of fading into the background with the other women who spend their days ferrying rich old ladies to card games, doctor's appointments, and special exhibitions at the MET. In the months before I came to live with my great grandmother's friend, my world was so painful that at first the absence of pain was pure pleasure.

And if these days I occasionally feel like a doll tossed around by a spoiled child, that's as much my fault as Eloise's. I'm twenty-three years old. I'm not a scared teenager anymore. I'm a grown woman who is fully capable of standing up for herself.

I just…don't. I learned the hard way what happens when you bite the hand that feeds you. It bites back, leaving wounds that never completely heal.

"At least think about it?" Shane asks, breaking into my thoughts. "The offer isn't going to expire. You can take as long as you need."

"All right," I say, though I fully intend to put the offer out of my mind. I can't let Shane help me. I want to be her friend, not her charity case. Not to mention the fact that I couldn't live with the shame if I let her down.

If she and Jake went to all the trouble to give me a fresh start and I ended up not being able to turn my life around, I wouldn't be able to hold my head up around either of them ever again.

Better to stay as I am, where I am, and learn to make the best of it, I decide, and put it out of my mind.

But now, as Eloise screeches my name again

on this ice cold February morning, I can't keep my brain from drifting to Shane's offer.

What might my day be like today if I were in my own apartment? Would I have time for a walk through the winter wonderland outside before I went to work? Would I have friends to call to make plans for a snowman building contest before I headed to my community college classes?

There was a time when I won big at school. I skipped two grades, graduated high school at sixteen with a National Merit Scholarship, and landed a full ride to Rutgers University. I could be good at learning things again. I could get that degree in architecture, or something more practical that would allow me to earn a living wage faster. Maybe accounting. Or nursing.

Or you could put your diabolical math skills to use on Wall Street devising quantitative software programs. That way, when you've retired, you'll be able to use your corporate spoils to hire your own companion to treat terribly in your old age.

The thought makes my stomach churn.

I don't want to be a Wall Street shark, or torture innocent people in my old age. I just want to take ownership of my life and stop paying for a mistake I made when I was a kid.

It's time to stop hiding in Eloise's spare room and get back out into the world.

Except that I've never been out in the world. I went from my parents' house to this room in Eloise's. Even with Shane's help, there's a chance the world will take one look at me, open its jaws, and eat me alive.

Like a baby bunny. Or a marshmallow peep. Chomp, chomp, all gone.

I wrinkle my nose at the thought. I'm not a marshmallow peep. When I have to be, I can be brave. Even if, in the end, my bravery is for nothing.

In the spirit of bravery, I put on my clingy black sweater dress, the only item in my closet that could be considered even remotely sexy. I pair it with knee high boots, a necklace made of beads and copper Shane gave me for Christmas, and my cat eye glasses with rhinestones in the frame. This afternoon, I'm taking Eloise to the theater, but come five o'clock I'm officially off duty for the next twenty-four hours.

Maybe I'll take my clingy dress out for dinner somewhere nice. Maybe even hit one of those singles bars Jake, Shane's husband, assures me are the low-key kind, not the scary kind. I might live with an elderly widow, but that doesn't mean I have to be in bed alone by nine o'clock every night. And maybe giving dating another shot will build up my courage to make other changes.

If I can survive dating in Manhattan, applying for night school at a city college should be a breeze.

Feeling inspired for a day of brave things—or at least seriously considering brave things—I leave my room, treading softly on the thick hall carpet. Eloise detests the sound of feet "tromping like elephants" down her hallways. I was never a tromper, but after years in Eloise's employ, I move like a ninja, my steps whisper-quiet.

I'm making a mental note to add "ninja walk" to my list of job skills—you never know what an employer might be looking for—when I step into the kitchen to see Eloise parked in her usual spot in the breakfast nook, the phone book open on the table before her, and a hell-raising expression on her face.

Addie

"Good morning, Eloise." I move into the kitchen without delay, fetching the kettle from the burner and filling it at the sink.

Eloise has surprised me with the phonebook a few times before—usually when she's angry and compiling a list of Very Important People to call with a list of Demands and Criticisms—and the quickest way to defuse her is with a cup of hot tea.

"The goodness of the morning remains to be seen. I've already had to wait far too long for something to take the chill off," Eloise replies, even though I'm running five minutes ahead of schedule. She pushes her wire glasses higher on her nose. "Why must they make the print so small, Adeline? Does the phone company expect their patrons to have a magnifying glass on hand when they need to place a call?"

"What number are you looking for?" I put the kettle on and start arranging the tea things on the tray. "I can look it up online for you. Or you can borrow my cell if you would rather look it up yourself."

"Heavens, no. Do you want to give me a brain tumor?" Eloise looks up sharply. "Well, do you?"

"No, of course not. Don't be silly." My smile shrivels beneath her glare. Apparently she's been listening to her friend Claire's theories about cell phone radiation again and isn't in a joking mood. "Would you like me to look it up in the book for you, then?" I ask, changing tacks. "I have my glasses on."

"I can see that," Eloise snaps. "I'm not blind. I also have my glasses on, and my eyes work perfectly well." Her gaze sweeps up and down, taking in my dress and shiny black boots. "Expecting company for breakfast, are we?"

I force a smile and pin it in place this time, refusing to let her bad mood rain on my courage parade. "No, just looking forward to the theater later, so I thought I'd wear a dress. Dresses make things feel festive, don't you think?"

She huffs as she flips another whisper-thin page. "I thought you might be expecting Miss Willoughby's beau to stop by. You've certainly been fussing with yourself a lot more since that man moved in upstairs."

I frown but keep my tone light as I remind

her, "Miss Willoughby is Mrs. Falcone now. That man is her husband."

"Which makes the way you look at him even more scandalous," Eloise mutters.

I turn from the tray, propping a hand on my hip and pinning her with a glare. Unfortunately, she isn't looking at me. Her nose is still buried in the phone book, somewhere in the Rs, if I'm not mistaken.

"I have no idea what you're talking about," I say firmly. "Jake is my friend. Just like Shane is my friend. That's all there is to it."

Eloise hums, but she doesn't take her gaze from the tiny print. "Is that right? Well, my mistake, I suppose. But I'm certainly not mistaking the way you fawn all over that criminal down on eighty-sixth street."

"Do you mean Kevin?" I squint, trying to understand how we made the leap from Jake to a homeless man. It's too early for this much crazy, but Eloise does enjoy tormenting me before I've had caffeine.

"Which proves my point." She taps a finger emphatically on the page in front of her. "What decent young woman goes around learning the names of the local degenerates?"

"Kevin is homeless, Eloise. We don't know if he's a criminal or a degenerate." I spoon tea into the teapot filter with more force than necessary. "And when I speak to someone more than once or twice, I like to introduce myself. It's just good manners. Besides, the man quotes poetry—what's so horrible about that? Personally, I would rather treat people with dignity until given a reason to do otherwise. We don't know what Kevin's been through, and a little compassion can go a long way when you're down on your luck."

Eloise's brows crawl higher on her forehead, proving she's as surprised by my rant as I am. She meets my gaze, her blue eyes sharp and assessing, looking as if she's deciding where to skewer a particularly disappointing piece of black market meat. "I see. This is personal for you, isn't it?"

I'm on the verge of begging her to stop picking at me until I've had a cup of tea, when the pot begins to whistle, and I lunge for the handle like a lifeline. I'm five minutes of steeping away from a cup of earl grey, which I will drink as soon as it's cool enough to suck down, Eloise's perfect temperature be damned.

"Because of your situation," Eloise continues as I fill the pot, put the lid on, and cover it with a tea cozy. "With your parents and your...trouble."

I freeze, my skin going cold. She's never talked about my parents or the reason I came to live with her, not once in all these years.

"I don't know what you mean," I whisper, my stomach tying itself in an elaborate knot.

"Well, if I hadn't taken you in, *you* might be homeless," Eloise says, her matter-of-fact words a knife slid neatly between my ribs. "You could have been out there on the streets with your poet, begging for change."

I shake my head, silently denying it, though she's probably right.

Maybe if Mom had known I had nowhere else to go, she would have let me come home. But maybe she wouldn't have. The not knowing is a cold wind that blows straight through my heart, and Eloise is clearly relishing holding open the door.

"But personal or not, this can't be allowed to continue." She sniffs, lifting her pointy nose into the air. "I was up all night thinking about how you encourage that man, making him think you're friends on the way to something more. It's scandalous."

"Eloise, that's ridiculous! I've never—"

"And dangerous!" She lifts her hands into the air in surrender, as if *I'm* the one attacking her first thing in the morning. "What happens when he decides talking isn't enough for him anymore? When he decides to follow you back here and make himself at home in my kitchen?"

"We have a doorman to let him know he isn't on the visitor's list," I remind her. "But there's no reason to think that Kevin would—"

"There are ways around that doorman, as you very well know." She wags an energetic finger, making me suspect she had Mina pop out and pick her up a cappuccino before I woke up. She's way too sassy for having been deprived of tea since her cup of Sandman's Friend last night.

"The woman who kidnapped Miss Willoughby walked right past Aaron with a *gun* and the man didn't even notice. Not to mention the fact that he allowed a madwoman who wasn't on the approved list to get up to the penthouse in the first place. There are flaws in our security, and until we implement new procedures, none of us are safe. This isn't the time to start making dangerous friends and courting disaster!"

I drop two sugar cubes into my cup with a sigh. "Eloise, please. I'm not courting disaster. I'm saying hello to a nice old man. Don't you think you're blowing this out of proportion?"

Her mouth prunes, and I do my best not to think uncharitable thoughts about how much her lips look like a cat's anus. "The only thing I may be blowing out of proportion is your continued usefulness. If I can't trust my companion to keep me safe, then what's the point in continuing to pay your salary, Adeline? Answer me that if you're so clever this morning!"

It's the first time she's flat out threatened to fire me instead of inferring it with a sneaky, passive aggressive comment to one of her friends about the "difficulty of finding dependable help."

Strangely, hearing the words spoken aloud is almost a relief.

"Well, that's a choice you have to make," I say, calmly stirring my tea. "You have every right to let me go, but I promise that I have always done my best to take care of you, and I'm happy to continue doing so. I don't believe Kevin is a threat to your safety or to mine, but if you're so worried that it's keeping you awake at night, I can explain to him that my employer would rather I not speak to him while I'm at work. Will that solve the problem?"

She shakes her head briskly. "No, that won't do at all. You'll make him angry if you do that. Honestly, girl, have you no common sense at all?"

I fight the urge to throw my hands in the air. "Then how would you suggest I handle it? There's no way around that corner unless we go a long block out of our way every time we cross the street into the park."

"We won't have to go around it." Her lips curve into a mean little grin as she taps a finger on the phonebook. "We'll get rid of the nuisance, instead. I'm going to call Eunice's son, the one who works with the district attorney's office. We'll explain to him that this vagrant has been harassing us, saying rude things and threatening violence, and they'll pop over and have him taken away."

My mouth opens and closes twice before I can recover enough to form words. "But that's not true."

She sniffs. "It doesn't matter if it's true. I'll have my peace of mind, and the man will be better off in a mental ward than out on the street. That's all you care about, isn't it, Adeline? Your friend's well-being?"

"No, it's not." I shake my head, still having a hard time believing she's serious. "And I won't lie about someone to the police."

"District attorney," she corrects me.

"Or the district attorney or anyone else! That's against the law, Eloise. And Kevin is a person, not a piece of garbage you can have taken away."

"Don't mock me, Adeline," she says, her voice hard. "You have a choice to make. Either take the necessary steps to eliminate the threat you've introduced into my life, or remove yourself from it. I made a promise to your father when you were a girl, little miss, but you're not a girl anymore." Her thin lip curls. "And I'm beginning to believe I've indulged your eccentricities long enough."

My jaw drops so hard the joint cracks. "*My* eccentricities? *Mine?* This from the woman who sent me to buy sheep's cheese that's deliberately infected with maggots?"

"It's a delicacy," she says, her spine going stiff.

"It's illegal in the United States, Eloise. And *maggots*. Maggots!"

"I suppose I can't blame you for your lack of sophistication," she says, mouth pruning again. "I knew what I was in for when I hired a teenager from the middle of nowhere, New Jersey, to be my companion. No matter how intelligent you were alleged to be, I should have known a girl who lied to her parents and—"

"No!" I point a shaking finger at her spiteful

face. "You don't get to tell me who I am or what I'm worth. *I* decide those things. And I've decided that I quit. Right now."

"What?" Eloise sputters, her eyes growing comically wide. "You can't quit! You haven't given two weeks notice. Who's going to read the paper? You know Mina doesn't know a word of English."

"You should have thought about that before you were terrible," I say, heading for the front door instead of to my room to pack my things. Now that I've finally decided to leave, I can't wait another moment. I need to be out of this house, away from the stale, Eloise-tainted air. Out in snow where the crisp winter day still has possibilities left in it. "I'll send someone to pick up my things."

"You will not!" Eloise wheels out from behind the table, moving swiftly under her own power for the first time in recent memory, proving she isn't nearly as frail as she pretends to be. "I will not have you sending strangers to my home! I'll toss your belongings out on the stoop first."

"Then toss away." I storm into the foyer, throwing open the hall closet. "Or I'll pay Mina to take my things to Shane's place. Whichever gives you the most miserable pleasure, Eloise, because Lord knows that's what you're all about, isn't it?"

"Terrible!" Eloise rolls into the foyer, stopping with one hand pressed to her heart. "Terrible,

terrible girl! How dare you? After all I've done for you!"

I shrug my coat on and wrap my scarf around my neck with swift whips of my arm. "You're right. After all you've done, I have no idea why it took you threatening an innocent man to make me leave. I guess it proves that I worry more about other people than I do myself. But that stops now. I deserve kindness, too, Eloise. I deserve an employer who offers a kind word now and then, or who at least remembers that I'm allergic to shellfish before ordering a potentially lethal Christmas dinner for the third year in a row."

Eloise makes a bleating sound, but I don't let her get a word in.

"But then, you probably did that on purpose, didn't you?" A laugh bursts from my chest as I hook my purse over my shoulder and dig inside for my keys. "Just for the fun of seeing me puff up like a balloon when I took a bite of macaroni and cheese before realizing there was lobster in it."

I find my key ring and pop the key to Eloise's apartment free from the rest, holding it up in the air between us. "Well, I hope that was enjoyable for you, but I'm removing myself from the 'people you get to bully' list. Good bye, Eloise." I drop the key to the carpet, then spin and slam out the door, ignoring her shrill demand that I come back and explain myself.

I think I've explained myself just fine.

And with every step I take toward the elevator, I feel lighter, freer, and…angrier. Angry at Eloise, at my family, and at Nate for getting to walk away from me without a scratch, while every dream I had withered and died.

I'm angry at myself, too—self-hatred is a hobby I've indulged in for too long to give it up cold turkey—but this new anger I've let out of its cage is hot enough to make me feel ten feet tall and bulletproof. I'm so fired up that I skip the elevator and pound down the stairs to the lobby, feeling like I'll explode if I don't burn up some of the energy.

I burst through the doors and storm past Aaron at the desk, not bothering to respond to his call for me to have a nice day.

It won't be a *nice* day, but it's going to be a memorable one. It's the first day of the rest of my life, and damn it, I'm going to do something to mark the occasion.

Whipping my phone from my purse, I jab out a quick text to Shane.

Is that room you double-booked still available? If you haven't found someone to take it yet, I would love to. Turns out I'm able to get five days off in a row, after all.

Shane and Jake—being Shane and Jake—both booked a surprise trip for their first Valentine's Day together, which meant deciding between five days at a sprawling Victorian lodge in the Catskills or seven days in Paris. Paris won, and Shane and

Jake are headed to the airport later today.

But Shane is an early riser, and I'm not surprised when my phone pings a few seconds later.

It's available! I'll email the details now! Yay, I'm so excited for you! Did Eloise get visited by the ghosts of Valentine's Day past last night or something? How on earth did you get her to give you a real vacation?

Setting off down the street toward the subway to Queens, where I remember seeing a place offering affordable rental cars during one of my many obscure-food-hunting missions, I type a reply.

She didn't. I quit. I walked out a few minutes ago with my purse, coat, and nothing else. I'm going to ask Mina to pack my things and drop them at your place, if that's okay. If you can pay her for her trouble, I'll pay you back. I'm sorry to be a bother, but I couldn't stay there another minute.

My phone starts to ring almost immediately, but I don't answer Shane's call. She'll want to talk, and I can't right now. I can't do anything but keep going, keep moving, keep running until I get away from the sad, small, shadowed life I've been living. Far enough away that I can look in the mirror and see someone other than a girl who messed up her life and let it stay that way.

I text Shane one last time: *Thank you so much for everything, but I can't talk. Not yet.* Then I turn off my phone.

I'm lucky to have a friend like Shane, but right

now I need to be on my own, just me and my thoughts and a ninety-mile drive to a place that's hopefully far enough away that I'll be able to figure out what happens next.

Nate

I'm no stranger to going to extremes for my work.

A few years ago, I lived in an igloo for a month while researching an article on social media detox. I slept with pack dogs to stay warm, peed in a tin can to avoid going outside in minus-forty-degree temperatures, and slowly went sane as Internet withdrawal gave way to an enlightening experience about how rich time becomes when you spend it wisely. Then there was the week I ate nothing but insects as a promotional stunt for a book I co-wrote on combatting world hunger, the month I lived on frequent flier miles, the gig as a professional castle-sitter, and my many trips to the creepiest corners of the world in search of inspiration for my annual volume of short fiction, *Fear, in Brief.*

For years, I've cobbled together a career writing this and that, drafting first and praying later that there would be a market for "You Probably Think This Article is About You: Narcissism in the Digital Age."

Now, I finally have a contract, a fat advance, and eighteen months to spend writing and researching *Faking It: Living Lies, Getting By, and Seeing How Far Moxie will Really Take You.* I've already faked my way through a week as a stockbroker, ten days as a lion handler, a weekend as a motivational speaker to Nine Lifers—people who believe they are reincarnations of ancient Egyptian cats. For real. These people exist and are allowed to vote, own guns, and stand next to you in the line at Starbucks—and another month-long stint as a tattoo artist.

Compared to inking a permanent mistake on someone's body, or being mauled to death by lions, helping people get revenge on their evil exes should be a piece of cake. And my first fake boyfriend gig for Magnificent Bastard Consulting *was* pretty damned easy. I helped a sweet older woman get back at the man who'd broken her heart—and stolen priceless pieces of art from her collection—and walked away with ten grand and a surprising sense of well-being.

I should have quit as soon as the job wrapped, and gotten busy drafting. My research is done, and it's time to make the damned words. But turns out writing long form non-fiction isn't nearly as much fun as the horror novels I've been penning and not selling for the past few years. And that damned "getting one over on the bad guy" thing sucked me in.

Working as an intervention expert at MBC was the first fake job that left me feeling good. And who doesn't like to feel good, like the work you're doing is more meaningful than a gimmick to sell a book you're not that excited about writing in the first place?

So I signed on for another case.

And another, figuring I could fit my writing in around helping people in need.

And now, four months later, my word count is in the shitter, and I'm headed to a mountain lodge with a lovely gentleman who insists I'm going to make his evil ex, Max, eat his heart out with envy. I'm not so sure—I'm not gay, haven't patted another guy's ass since I gave up football after high school, and have zero experience pretending to be in love with another dude.

Chances are I'm going to let Eduardo down in a spectacular fashion. Faking it until you make it is all well and good, but I might as well have "colorblind straight guy" tattooed on my forehead. Even with wardrobe help from Ed, I'm going to be hard pressed to convince anyone I'm batting for the other team, especially a guy like Max, who's been in intimate relationships with men for longer than I've been alive.

Eduardo's ex is going to see right through me,

and these five days away from my computer and piece of shit Chapter Five—fuck you, Chapter Five, you fucking eternal pain in my ass—will have been for nothing.

Add in the fact that this is the first time I've been back to the Catskills since Addie and I spent that last, magical day together at Yankee Lake and I'm as far from cool and collected as I've been in years. I'm closer to "Hot Fucking Mess," which is hardly the Magnificent Bastard Eduardo requested.

"Relax, cupcake." Ed claps me on the back as I take the turn leading up to Tomahawk Mountain House, the luxury resort where we'll be spending a long Valentine's Day weekend. "Everything is going to be fine."

"Shouldn't I be the one putting you at ease?" I ask, willing my fingers to relax their death grip on the wheel.

"I don't need to be put at ease. I just need to see the look on Max's face when I walk into the dining room with you on my arm while you're wearing those jeans." Ed rubs his perfectly manicured hands together with a wicked laugh. He's nearly as tall as my six feet two, with the barrel-chested build common in some older men, but his polished appearance and head full of black hair make him look younger than fifty-five. "If he doesn't turn puce with envy, I'll eat my body weight in that hideous hair gel he invented."

"Puce," I echo with a smile. "Much nastier

than green."

"Oh, it is, doll face. It's going to be *uuuugly*. You're exactly his type—dark hair, strong jaw, and cheekbones a supermodel would sell her kidneys for. Honest to God, you're almost as handsome as I was when I was your age."

I laugh. "Thanks, man."

He tsks. "No 'man' or 'dude.' Too bro-mancy. Just call me Ed, or Eddie."

I nod, anxiety creeping back in to tighten my shoulders. "Right. Sorry."

"Stop apologizing, Prince Charming, I know this is your first time running the game with a mister instead of a sister. I'm not expecting you to medal in the Rainbow Olympics your first time out."

"I appreciate that." I ease off the gas, slowing as the road winds higher through dense forests of evergreens and patches of ice begin to dot the pavement.

"And like I said yesterday," Eduardo continues. "Max and I are from another generation. Back when we were starting our adventure, it wasn't always safe for two men to show affection in public. And we're going to a mountain lodge, not a gay bar, for Christ's sake. A little hand holding and a few steamy looks will be enough to convince Max you're my new honeybun, no bumping and grinding on the dance floor required." He nudges my shoulder with a gentle fist. "So, is that enough pep talk, doll? Feeling better yet?"

"Much better, thanks. And I promise I'll do my best not to let you down."

Eduardo hums appreciatively beneath his breath. "How on Earth have you managed to stay single, Nathaniel? Sweet as pie *and* easy on the eyes? I would think the ladies would be oiling up to bikini wrestle in the kiddie pool for a guy like you."

"I move around a lot," I say with a laugh, because it's easier than admitting that I suck at relationships. That I always have. Except for that one summer, and who knows how that would have turned out. It probably would have ended badly.

Addie and I were too fucking young. Too young to know what love really was, let alone how to make it last.

"And I'm not always so well put together," I add with a self-deprecating grin. "Thank you again for supplying my wardrobe."

"One of the perks of having friends in the fashion industry, doll. Besides, Max knows I'm too vain to allow my beautiful boy toy to run around in something off the rack." Ed shudders, presumably at the thought of wearing retail. "Though it's a shame we have to cover so much of you up. Have I mentioned that I hate winter? Skiing is Max's thing. I'm a beach and mojito man myself."

He reaches out to crank up the heat. The

higher we go, the colder the air gets, making me glad the rest of my Eduardo-selected clothes are as warm as the gray cashmere sweater, Egyptian cotton button-down, and flannel-lined jeans I'm wearing. He's outfitted me for everything from skiing, to winter hiking, to hanging around the lodge drinking hot cocoa and looking good on his arm. I've got more luggage in the trunk than my mother and sister bring when they come to visit for a long weekend.

"What about you? Sand or snow? What's your pleasure?" Ed asks, but before I can confess I'm a fan of winter, he gasps and points a finger at the road ahead, where a slender woman in a dark coat is wrestling a tire out of the trunk of her car.

"Oh, the poor thing." Eduardo lays a hand on my forearm. "She must be freezing to death. Take it from a man who's spent his share of time in drag, sheer pantyhose do nothing to hold in body heat. We should pull over and help the lamb before she gets frostbite."

I had already planned to stop, but it's good to know that Eduardo is as nice as he seems. It makes me even more determined to give this intervention my A game and teach his piece of shit ex that cheating on your spouse while trying to stage a hostile takeover of his hair salon empire doesn't pay.

I pull to the side of the road in front of the woman's beat up Chevy and shove the car into park. Before I can turn the key, Eduardo leans in to whisper, "This means you're on, doll. There isn't much else on this godforsaken mountain, so I'm guessing our damsel in distress is headed up to the lodge. We don't want to blow our cover before we get there."

"Got it. I'm in hopelessly devoted mode, Ed," I say with a wink. "From now until the day we head home, bathed in victory and Maxwell's tears."

Eduardo laughs. "Oh, I love it! I'm usually a shower man, but I can't wait to soak in a big vat of those." He's still chuckling as we get out of the car and turn to the woman waving a gloved hand in our direction.

"Hey," she says, relief clear in her high, sweet, way too fucking familiar voice. "I'm headed to the lodge, but my spare is flat, and I…"

Her words trail off as her gaze connects with mine. Our eyes meet, and her jaw drops, her lips forming a horrified O that makes it clear she isn't glad to see me.

But why the hell would she be?

Still, I can't help being happy to see her. More than happy. She takes my fucking breath away, the way she always did. Looking into her shining blue eyes, it feels like no time has passed, like I'm still that stupid kid who believed forever fell into your lap and love was meant to be easy. I take one look at her and Adeline happens to me all over again, the way she did before.

Except this time, she hates me.

Fuck, she hates me, and I hate that she hates me.

I have to explain. I have to apologize. I have to make her believe that I never intended to break my promises or her heart.

My lips part, but before any words can find their way out into the cold air, Eduardo hurries around me with his arms outstretched. "There, there, no need to cry, sweetheart. I'm Eduardo and this is my boyfriend, Nate, and we're happy to give you a ride to the lodge. We're staying there, too!" He pulls Addie into his arms, hiding her face in his chest as he murmurs, "Don't worry, precious. We're going to save the day and get you in out of the cold. Isn't that right, Prince Charming?"

Fuck me again.

Eduardo is right. Until this job is done, I'm his Prince Charming, and explaining myself to Addie, begging for forgiveness, or telling her that she's even more beautiful than I remembered are all off the table.

"That's right." I force the words out through a throat so tight it feels like I'm getting a hug from a boa constrictor.

"Thank you," Addie mumbles, but she doesn't move out of Eduardo's arms or look my way.

The Adeline I knew wasn't the kind to accept hugs from strangers. But maybe she's changed. Or maybe Eduardo gives really good hugs. Or maybe she's so traumatized by seeing me again that she's willing to settle for any comfort in the cold.

She has every reason to despise me. She doesn't know what was at stake or how hard I tried to find her. She doesn't know that loving her is the truest thing I've ever done, or that leaving her is my number one regret. Full stop.

So tell her, asshole!

You finally have a chance to make things right. If you let it slip through your fingers this time, there will be no one to blame but yourself.

My hands curl at my sides as I silently vow to make this right. I owe Addie the truth, and whatever comfort might come from knowing that I never meant to turn my back on her.

Looking at her now, though, with her forehead on Eduardo's chest and her skin so pale, I wonder if that makes a damned bit of difference. Cut off a person's hand on purpose or by accident, the result is exactly the fucking same.

Chapter SIX

Adeline

The world is spinning, and my head feels like it's been invaded by a swarm of very angry, very confused bees.

I can't believe this is happening. I can't believe that *Nate* pulled over to help me. *Nate*, and his very nice boyfriend, Eduardo, who gives absolutely spectacular papa-bear hugs.

His boyfriend, Eduardo.

His *boyfriend*.

Oh my God…

Oh my flipping God…

The swarm of bees clears, and I step out of Eduardo's very nice smelling arms. "Good to see you again, Nate." The words sound forced, but I'm resisting the urge to flip him the bird and scream that I would rather be stranded on the road forever than accept a ride from him.

So that's good. Or at least a start, anyway.

"You two know each other?" Eduardo's dark brows furrow as he glances over his shoulder at his boyfriend.

His *boyfriend*. Oh my God. Will that ever not be totally weird?

"Addie and I were friends in high school." Nate moves closer with that smooth, confident stride of his, the one that made it so easy to believe he was some pretty devil who'd crawled out of the hellmouth to tempt me into losing my way.

He still walks like an athlete and looks even more like a supermodel than he used to. My clothes come from thrift stores and fifty-percent off sales at the Bargain Basement, but I've spent years surrounded by obscenely rich people. I know the cut and texture of very expensive clothes, and the outfit Nate is wearing probably cost more than I make in a year.

And he looks *damned* good in it, too, damn him. So good—*damn it, damn it, damn it*—that it's hard to think, to swallow, to continue to breathe without gulping like a landed fish.

But somehow I manage to say, "After high school, really. We were summer friends."

"What an amazing coincidence!" Eduardo's eyes widen dramatically. "What are the odds, darling?" He chuckles as he reaches out, twining his fingers through Nate's. "But you know what this means, don't you, Prince Charming?"

I stare at their joined hands and the swarm of confused bees takes another spin through my head, making my temples ache.

"It means I'm about to get some good gossip," Eduardo continues in a teasing tone. "I can't wait to hear the dirt, Addie darling. I insist you tell me all about baby Nate and how good he looked in his football uniform. I've heard he was a star back in the day."

Nate clears his throat. "Actually, Adeline never—"

"I never saw him play," I cut in, forcing my gaze from their hands to Eduardo's kind face. "We weren't that close, actually."

I can't look at Nate right now, not when I'm still reeling from the shock of seeing those melt-your-heart brown eyes for the first time in years, not to mention realizing that the only man I've ever loved is gay.

Nate is *gay*. Gay. Dicks over chicks, penis over Venus, "No thanks, Vagina, I'll have my love with a side of dick" gay.

Jesus Christ, how could I not have known? Sure, I was a kid with no experience, but there hadn't been the slightest sign.

Had there?

I rack my brain, trying to make sense of what Eduardo is saying as he guides me toward the BMW parked in front of my rent-a-wreck, while mentally combing through every moment of that summer with Nate, looking for clues I could have missed. But there isn't anything, except maybe my own boyish, sixteen-year-old figure. Hell, Nate thought I was a kid when we first met. I was barely a B cup with help from my very best bra, and so slim that in a ball cap and a baggy tee I probably looked as much like a boy as a girl.

The year I graduated, I had a hell of a time keeping on weight. I'd shot up three inches in twelve months, which probably contributed to—

I shut the thought down, cutting it off like the head of a snake coiling to strike. I don't think about *that*, ever, and certainly not when I'm within spitting distance of Nate.

"You don't have any suitcases, Addie?" Nate asks.

My name sounds so wonderfully, terribly familiar on his lips that I have to fight to keep the misery it inspires from my face as I turn to tell him, "No, no suitcases."

"Oh. Okay." His expression as he slams the trunk of my rental car is intense and concerned and so totally *inappropriate* that I'm tempted to throw a rock at his face. But the side of the road is covered with snow—evil snow that hides all the good rocks that I could be grabbing if it weren't winter.

"No luggage?" Eduardo clucks kindly as he pats my shoulder. "You've been through something, haven't you, dear?"

"Nothing too bad. Just decided to take a last minute trip," I say, because I refuse to let Nate know how shitty my life has been lately. I don't want him to know anything about me, except that I am super, awesome, amazingly fine without him.

"But things are looking up," I add with forced chipperness. "Thank you both for being so sweet. I really appreciate it, and would love a ride up to the lodge."

"Absolutely! Life can be a bitch, but sometimes she sends us help when we need it." Eduardo pats my back again, his touch surprisingly comforting. It's been a while since a father-figure type has shown me kindness. It's nice, even if Eduardo is sleeping with the only man I've ever slept with.

You and Eduardo have both touched Nate's penis. Probably more than touched it…

The thought, unexpectedly, makes me giggle.

"Atta girl!" Eduardo cheers. "Laughter is the best medicine."

"It is," I agree, reaching for the door to the backseat. I'm still tittering when Nate slides into the driver's seat, filling the car with his irresistible Nate smell.

"You okay?" he asks, glancing over his shoulder.

"Awesome." I bite my lip and nod, forcing myself to shut down the giggle fest. But inside, I'm still down on the ground, rolling. I'm in a laugh or cry situation, and considering I already wasted a year of my life crying over Nate, laughter is clearly the better option.

Now I just have to make it up to the lodge without embarrassing myself, so I can retreat to my room, laugh until I throw up, and figure out what I'm going to do about being stranded at a romantic mountain hideaway with my ex-lover, his new boyfriend, and a hundred or so other couples who will do their best to remind me that I am single and alone and that Eduardo's friendly hug was the most action I've gotten in so long that I can't think about it without wanting to jump out of the car and start looking for rocks again.

So I don't think.

I smile and listen to Eduardo talk about the weather and the storm that could be headed in tomorrow and how much he hates snow. I agree that spending the weekend in the spa sounds smart and pretend I can't feel Nate's soulful gaze on me in the rearview mirror. I survive the final ten miles up to the lodge the way I've survived the past seven years—by staying in the moment, taking one shitty second at a time, and never, ever looking back.

Because the past is a predator hot on your heels. It's just waiting for you to stop and look back, to slow down enough that it can pounce, dig in its claws, and rip your stupid, naïve, maybe-things-will-get-better head off.

Chapter SEVEN

From the text archives of Adeline "Addie
Klein and Shane Willoughby Falcone

Addie: Shane, are you awake? I have no idea what
time it is in Paris, but I REALLY need to talk to
you. Really, really, REALLY bad.

Shane: Yeah, I'm awake. How's it going, babe?

Addie: Um, not too good.
Nate is here, Shane. He's here at the lodge with
his boyfriend!
Yes, you read that right. His BOYFRIEND.
They picked me up on the side of the road after
my rental car broke down and gave me a ride to
the lodge, where they are both staying for the
entire five days that I'm here. Both of them.
Together.
In the same room, because they are

BOYFRIENDS and in love and Eduardo wants
them to adopt a puppy together, one that has
Nate's hazelnut eyes and Eduardo's curly black
hair and NO I am not making any of this up!!

Shane: Crazy.
You should come see me at the bar.

Addie: What? You're in Paris.
And did you see what I wrote up there?
About Nate and his boyfriend? HIS
BOYFRIEND?!!!!

Shane: Some guys like other guys, Adeline. No
need to get your panties in a twist about it.
Speaking of panties…are you wearing any?

Addie: What?!!

Shane: How about a bra? Wearing one of those?
I could go for a tit shot right now.

Addie: Who the hell is this?!

Shane: I'm Shane, your boyfriend.
Come see me at the cocktail club on Rue Saint-
Sauveur
Bring your tits ☺.

Addie: Shane is a woman, asshole. And SHE has
no interest in my tits!

Now take this phone back to wherever you found it right now! Stealing someone's phone and texting their friends is a jerk move. Not to mention illegal!

Shane: You texted me. I was just trying to be polite.

Addie: By asking for pictures of my tits?!

Shane: You're the one that hates gay people, lady. You should get therapy before you commit a hate crime.
Love is love, sister.

Addie: I'm not going to commit a hate crime! Nate is my ex-boyfriend, that's why I'm upset that he's gay. I have nothing against gay people. At all. Not even a little bit.

Shane: I think you protest too much.

Addie: Well, I think you're a thief so I don't care what you think!!!

Shane: That's an awful lot of exclamation points for someone who doesn't care.
You seem pretty high strung, Adeline Klein.
I don't think I want a picture of your tits, after all…

Addie: MY TITS WERE NEVER ON THE TABLE!

Shane: And to be honest, I don't get why you're so upset about your ex being gay. Isn't that a good thing?

Addie: What?!

Shane: Well, he's your ex, so that clearly means it didn't work out.
And seeing how high strung and against showing your tits you are, I'm guessing he broke things off with you. Am I right?

Addie: He didn't break up with me. He told me he loved me, and that he was changing schools to be with me because I was more important to him than anything else in the world, and then he left town without even saying good-bye.
No explanation. Not even "just kidding, Addie, ha, you got played!"
Just gone. Bam. Vanished.
No forwarding number, no Dear Jane letter, no nothing. He went off to pledge a fraternity and drink beer like we'd never quoted Einstein or fallen in love or had the most magical, beautiful, perfect summer in the history of summers.

Shane: Wow, that's a total dick move.
But well… Maybe he was dealing with some

heavy shit, too.

Addie: Like what?

Shane: Maybe he was coming to terms with the fact that he was gay. That can be pretty fucking painful, you know. It's not like society or your family or anyone else really makes it easy for people to come out of the closet. They want you to stay stuffed in there, so they can keep saying that equal rights only belong to straight, white people.

Addie: Okay, listen, I get your point, but—

Shane: Do you really? Have you ever had to deal with anything like that?
Do you know what it feels like for your father to tell you he would have cut off your dick when you were a baby if he'd known what you were going to grow up to be?
Take a second and check your privilege, Adeline.

Addie: Check *your* privilege! Being a woman in this society isn't always a super fun joy ride either. And I've had to deal with more than my share of that.
But why am I even talking to you?
You're a jerk stranger who stole my friend's phone and asked me if I was wearing panties.
You are not to be trusted or taken seriously!!

Shane: I didn't steal it. I found it on a bench. And sometimes strangers give the best advice. A stranger helped me find the guts to quit my job and travel the world.
I'm living my dream because of a stranger.
Now it's my turn to help.
Let me help, Adeline. I'm sorry I asked you about your panties.
(Not sorry about the bra, though, gotta keep it real.)

Addie: Sigh…
Is this day from hell ever going to end?

Shane: I'm serious! Let me help you.
Here's why you should feel better now that you know your ex is gay:
This guy didn't love you and leave you because you're not lovable. He cut and ran because he needed something from a romantic relationship that you could never give. And that something was a DICK, Adeline, and all the other stuff that goes along with it. It wasn't your fault. You just happened to be born without the right equipment.

Addie: Ugh. You're just…
I can't even…

Shane: And maybe he bailed BECAUSE he cared about you. Think about that.

Maybe he knew he wouldn't be able to give you what you needed, either—a straight guy to be hetero-normative with and shit—so he ghosted before it was too late.

Addie: But it was already too late.
But… I don't know…
I guess he didn't know that.

Shane: You guess?

Addie: I know.
I know that he didn't.
The really bad stuff happened after he was already gone.

Shane: See there? So he was innocent. Maybe. Either way, you've got a load off your shoulders. Because you can't turn someone gay. I promise. No matter how often you refuse to talk about your panties or send sexy pics.

Addie: You're kind of funny.

Shane: Does that mean you're going to send me something sexty?
I promise I won't share it with anyone. I'll just brag about it.
A lot.
Like pretty much all the time.

Addie: This conversation is over.
I'm calling Shane's hotel and telling her to stop service on her cell phone.

Shane: Tell her to call Hillary while you're at it. She texted a little while ago about some charity thing—and was quite willing to show her tits, I'll add.

Addie: Hillary is ninety years old.

Shane: Yes, she is. I'm going to need about a gallon of bleach to get that shot out of my head, but I guess that's what I get for being a phone-stealing asshole.

Addie: I guess so. Good-bye, Pervert in Paris.

Shane: Good-bye, Adeline. And good luck.
It's all going to work out. I promise.
And if it doesn't, we'll all be dead soon anyway.

Addie: The worst…
The very, very worst…

Chapter EIGHT

Adeline

Virginia Wolf once said, "I ransack libraries and find them full of sunken treasure."

I've found more than my share of treasure in libraries. I've also found peace in times of struggle, hope in times of despair, and windows into worlds bigger than my own. When I need to remember that the world is full of small, stubborn light giving the middle finger to the darkness, I head to a library. And thankfully, Tomahawk Mountain House has a lovely lending library on the top floor.

I step out of the elevator and into a safe place, crossing thick carpet patterned with tribal symbols sketched in silver and gold. The floor to ceiling bookshelves, roaring fire in the stone fireplace, and plush couches and chairs arranged to offer readers privacy, immediately put me at ease.

The view isn't too shabby, either.

Two picture windows frame a stunning vista of the frozen lake and the snow-capped mountains beyond. In the distance, speck-sized skiers swish along downy drifts of snow, while closer in, skaters in hats and heavy coats circle an ice rink at the top of the first rise. I couldn't bring myself to focus long enough to read my entire welcome packet, but I believe it said something about free skate rental and a night skate under the stars coming up soon.

Normally, I would jump at the chance to get back in skates, but that was before Nate and Eduardo and my disturbing textual encounter with a pervert stranger somewhere in Paris.

A maybe sort of wise pervert stranger…

Maybe?

I settle into a loveseat near the windows, kick off my boots, and wonder what the perv's story is, because that's easier than wondering about other things.

I used to love making up stories for strangers when I was a kid, back when I thought I might be a novelist as well as an architect, a senator, and an inventor of interesting gadgets to use around the kitchen. At fifteen, I had no doubt that I could do anything I set my mind to. I was sheltered, coddled, and completely clueless as to how easily a big, fat eraser named Nate Casey could smudge out all my dreams.

Be fair. He did a terrible, hurtful thing, but he wasn't the eraser. Not really.

I sigh. It's true. My mother was the eraser. And the more I think about what the Paris Pervert said, the more I think it might make sense.

Back when it all went down, my gut kept screaming that Nate was coming back, that he wouldn't have left me the way he did unless he had a very good reason. Maybe being gay and scared of how his family, friends, and *girlfriend* would react to the news was that reason. Judging from Nate's stories, his father certainly wasn't the tolerant sort. He was the kind to send his son to one of those barbaric camps where they try to torture the gay out of people with electroshock therapy.

I shudder at the thought.

Maybe Nate truly felt he had no other choice but to run without telling me the truth. Maybe he was afraid I would be cruel to him, too. And maybe I would have been. I would have been angry, that's for sure. I would have wanted to know why he couldn't have figured out that he was gay before he took my virginity, made me love him, and became the only thing that felt right in the crazy, mixed-up world.

Looking out at the mountains, I can't help but think about our last trip together, of making love to him until it felt like we were the same person and I saw my forever right there in his eyes.

My heart is beating faster, fresh sadness and

confusion ramping up my beats per minute, when a familiar voice says, "I thought I might find you here."

I turn, a too-loud sound of disgust escaping from my lips before I can stop it, earning a sad face from Nate and a dirty look from the woman perusing the shelves on the far side of the room.

"I deserve that." He circles the couch, his hands shoved deep in his pockets and his beautiful brow furrowed as he nods toward the empty half of the loveseat. "Can I sit?"

"Sure, of course. Sit," I say, though I'm not ready to be this close to him.

He's still stupidly beautiful, and so heartbreakingly familiar. His face is a song I sang a thousand times, until the lyrics were a part of me. And then he left and took the music away.

As Nate sits down, squishing the cushion enough to boost me into the air, I remember what it felt like to be loved by him. To share secrets and adventures and books, and kisses that lasted forever. I used to kiss his perfect lips until my mouth was bruised and the taste of him was my entire world. There was a time I could have lived on his kisses and never wanted for food, but those days are far away, and my heart feels so much older than twenty-three.

When I meet his eyes, I notice the gold flecks that used to dazzle me, and all I want is to go back. Back to the days before I knew his tenderness was a lie and his beauty was only skin deep. Even knowing the way it ends, if I could, I would turn back time and live that summer with him all over again, just for the chance to feel so completely at home in someone's arms.

And that hurts. So much.

It hurts to know I'm still so weak, so pathetic. As pathetic as sixteen-year-old Addie crying at the window, waiting for the knight in shining armor who was never going to show.

No, Pervert in Paris is wrong. Nate being gay doesn't make anything better. It doesn't change a damned thing. It doesn't change the fact that I loved him and he threw me away. Nothing can make that better. *Nothing*. Even if he bolted because he couldn't bring himself to have sex with me anymore—a thought that's pretty crushing, considering making love to him was the best thing to happen to my body in my entire stupid life—it doesn't matter.

I was a kind, decent human being. I was his friend, a kindred spirit who loved him, and the only person in his life who knew what he was talking about when he quoted Shakespeare or Einstein, and who believed he could make a living with the stories he wrote. I knew his dreams and his hopes and, I thought, his heart. And he knew mine.

The day he left, he *knew* it would tear me apart. But he did it anyway, which means Nate Casey has a capacity for cruelty I would never have imagined possible when he was mine, and no amount of coming-out stress makes that okay.

"I talked to Eduardo." He leans in, completely unaware that I'm thinking about stabbing him repeatedly in those intense eyes of his. "He's a good guy, and he said it was okay for me to—"

"He seems like a good guy," I snap, deciding it's time to pull the plug on this conversation. Nate may be ready to cheek-kiss and make up, but I'm not, and I doubt I'll ever be.

I stand, forcing a smile because I refuse to let him know that being near him is so painful, even after all these years. "You two seem good together. I'm glad you're happy."

No, I'm not!

I hate that you're happy, and I hate that you don't remember me the way I remember you. I hate that you don't still love me or hate me or feel some strong, strangulating emotion when you think my name.

And most of all, I hate that you get to walk through life without the memory of that summer carved into your soul like a scarlet letter.

And I do. I hate it so much I'm afraid my fantasy violence might find its way into the real world, and I might actually do something crazy like rake my nails down Nate's face.

But before the impulse can become action, a perky voice from the door to the library calls out, "Last chance for hokey-pokey around the Valentine's Day tree! Come join us on the ground floor and shake it all about! We're decorating sugar cookies after! Heart-shaped of course!"

The woman has a long brown ponytail and an oversized sweater with "I love LOVE!" scrawled across it in pink letters, and I wave at her like we're best friends. "I'll be right there! Thanks for reminding me!"

Hokey-pokey sounds like about as much fun as being bitten by zombies while endlessly riding the Small World ride at Disney for all eternity, but if it gets me away from Nate, I'll shake it all about until the cows come home.

"Of course!" Miss In Love With Love motions for me to follow her. "We can share an elevator and grab hot chocolate before we start!"

I glance down at Nate, looking at his chin instead of his perfect lips or heartbreaking eyes or those big, strong hands that used to know all the secret ways to make my body sing. "Gotta run. Have a great vacation."

Or not, I silently add as I grab my boots and scurry around the loveseat in my sock feet. I'm certainly not looking forward to my vacation as much anymore. I had been excited about skating, hiking, and drinking my weight in hot chocolate as one of the Tomahawk ice-gondolas ferried me around the frozen lake in front of the hotel, but now staying in my room for the next five days is sounding pretty good.

Pretty damned good.

And so I let Tiffany—the activities director with the deep-seated love for the hokey-pokey—lead me down to the lobby, but slip away as soon as her back is turned. I make it safely to my room, tuck myself into bed, and resolve to stay there until Tuesday.

Or maybe, if I can find a way to pay for it, forever.

Forever under the covers sounds pretty good right now.

So I pull the quilt over my head, turn off the lights, and go to sleep with the sun at around six o'clock, happy to forego food or drink or entertainment as long as I can sink into oblivion for a few hours and pretend this day never happened.

Chapter NINE

From the texts of Adeline Klein
and Pervert in Paris

Addie: Are you still there Pervert?

Pervert: I am. No luck getting ahold of your friend at her hotel?

Addie: Not yet, but I left a message. Your reign of terror could end any moment.

Pervert: Good to know. I better finish checking in with all of my friends in the States.
I threw my cell phone in a fountain the day I decided to quit my job, and calling cards are so much more expensive than I thought they would be.
Turns out ditching my Friends and Family plan wasn't the best idea I've had lately.

Addie: You're full of bad calls. Like about my ex. Him being gay doesn't change anything. You said it yourself—love is love.

Pervert: Okay…

Addie: So it doesn't matter if he didn't want to sleep with me anymore, or be my boyfriend. If he had really loved me, even as a friend, he wouldn't have done what he did. Friends don't abandon friends.

Pervert: I see your point. But we all make mistakes.
Except you, right? You're perfect?

Addie: Of course I'm not perfect! But I don't hurt the people I claim to love!

Pervert: We all hurt the people we love. It's human nature. No matter how hard we try to be good, we just can't help ourselves.

Addie: I refuse to believe that. I think humans can be better than our nature.
Love can make us better.
It should make us better, anyway…

Pervert: You're more interesting than I thought you'd be when we started texting. And you make

some valid points…
I think maybe I would like to see your tits after
all.

Addie: Oh for Pete's sake…
Why did I text you? What was I thinking?
I must be losing my flipping mind.

Pervert: You texted me because I'm guessing you
don't have anyone else to talk to except Shane.
But she has tons of people. Her phone has been
blowing up all night.
So maybe instead of feeling sorry for yourself, or
letting the past drag you down into the sad pit,
you should get out and make some new friends.
That way you won't have to text a creep you
don't even know.
Because maybe confiding in the jerk who took
your friend's phone and keeps asking for tit pics
isn't the best investment of your time, ya know?

Addie: I think you actually just made me feel
worse. Thanks a lot, Pervert.

Pervert: Would a dick pic make you feel better?

Addie: NO! NOT AT ALL!
UGH!! I'M TURNING OFF MY PHONE
RIGHT NOW!

Pervert: Good! You do you, Addie!

Get out there and live your life and—

Sender blocked.

Nate

Eduardo and I spend approximately seven hundred and ten hours in the dining room eating dinner, giving Max and his date—a homely kid who looks young enough to be Max's inbred grandson—plenty of opportunity to observe us being desperately in love and shamelessly decadent. Ed orders a two-hundred dollar bottle of wine, five courses, and multiple desserts, and I do my best to pretend I'm not constantly scanning the room for a glimpse of Addie.

I have to find her before she leaves. Find her, corner her, and pin her to the ground if that's what it takes to get her to hear me out.

The thought of pinning Addie to the floor, feeling her curvier-than-it-used-to-be body pressed against mine and her breath warm on my lips, makes me ache. It's been six months since my last hook-up with my fuck buddy, Emily, but sex deprivation isn't why I want to get Addie in my arms so badly.

I don't want to get my rocks off; I want to explain things the way I used to explain things to Adeline. I want to kiss her sweet mouth, worship her with my hands, hear her gasp as I press inside her and prove to her with every stroke of my cock that I never meant to hurt her. Addie and I could always talk, but some of our best conversations took place without saying a word. I know if I could get her clothes off and her lips on mine, I could convince her that what we had was real and that I still care about her so fucking much.

I suck at relationships, and I've screwed things up with Adeline beyond repair, but that doesn't mean I don't care about her. I will always care, because she will always be the first—and maybe the only—person who made me believe that love was something more than the saccharine stuff of country songs and those steamy romances my university roommate, Mitch, likes to read.

He says they relax him, while providing spank bank material he appreciates now that he's quit his job to wander the world. Turns out most women are turned off by the homeless vagabond thing. So instead of Eat, Pray, Loving across the continents, Mitch is Eat, Pray, Jerking Off.

During dinner, I tell Eduardo stories about Mitch and Becca, his little sister, who dropped out of school to start a sleepaway camp for grownups, doing my best to keep up my end of the conversation. Eduardo makes it easy for me, laughing at even my weakest jokes in between meaningful touches to my hand or shoulder.

Surprisingly, none of it feels strange. It's easy to enjoy Eduardo's company and not much harder to make enjoyment look like something more. By the time Max storms from the dining room shortly before we've finished dessert, followed by the pouting pool boy, who glares covetously at my designer suit jacket on his way past, Max's face is bright red.

Eduardo grins like the Cheshire Cat and murmurs, "Oh, I'm having so much fun already, doll. Ex-husband outrage is delicious. I could live on it."

"Then maybe we should have gone with four courses instead of five." I groan as I bring a hand to my stomach. "I'm stuffed. You're going to have to conquer dessert without me."

Ed sighs dreamily, propping his chin on his fist as he watches our waiter approach with a loaded tray. "Well, it's a sacrifice, darling, but one I'm willing to make."

"You're so brave." I play up the flirtation in my voice as our waiter sets out dessert, coffee, and a selection of ports Eduardo chose to compliment the chocolate in the lava cake and the maple-crusted crème brulée.

Ed presses a hand to his chest and nods

seriously. "I am brave. Practically a martyr, really." He thanks the waiter, adding in a softer voice as the older man walks away, "Give me half an hour then you can go hunting for your girl again, sweet pea. I just want to make sure Max is tucked in for the night first. He's usually not one to emerge from his lair after dinner, but just in case, we should linger a little longer."

"I'll stick with you tonight," I say, though I'm grateful for the offer, and Ed's willingness to let Addie in on our secret. "I doubt I'll have a shot at finding Adeline again until tomorrow. She's not much of a night owl, either."

Ed tsks as he digs into the lava cake. "So the woman at the front desk wouldn't connect a call to her room, then?"

"She couldn't find a Klein. Addie must be registered under another name."

"Do you think she's married?" Ed asks, his eyes widening.

"I don't think so," I say, though the thought had crossed my mind when the redhead at the front desk assured me there wasn't a Klein checked into the lodge. The thought inspired unexpected anger, jealousy, and then a wave of unhappiness at the idea of Addie promising forever to some faceless asshole who clearly hasn't made her happy.

"Well, I didn't see a ring, but that doesn't mean anything these days," Eduardo says. "Only about half of my younger friends wear their wedding bands on a regular basis. No one takes pride in being bagged and tagged anymore. It's sad, really. When Max and I were first married, I was so proud of my ring. It was this lovely, simple reminder that I was never going to be alone again."

I touch his hand. "You'll find someone, Ed. You're a good man. You deserve better than a douchebag who cheated on you with a weasel-faced pool boy."

He smiles sadly. "And don't forget suing me for ownership of the salons. Salons I built from the ground up with blood, sweat, tears, and so many hours with a blow-dryer in my hand I've got tennis elbow without ever having picked up a racket."

"Exactly. You deserve better, and you're going to find it. I truly believe that."

"I've said it once, and I'll say it again—you're sweet." He lifts his spoon, stabbing it at the air in front of us as his eyes narrow. "What if Addie is separated, too? Or going through a nasty divorce? Maybe that's why the poor thing was so upset. Maybe running into the boy who broke her heart in high school was just the rotten raisin on her shit sundae of a day."

"I guess it's possible." Again, I experience the urge to punch this nameless fuck who hasn't loved Addie the way he should have.

"In any case, you have to talk to her before she checks out, Nathaniel." Eduardo licks chocolate from his spoon and reaches for a glass of port. "Your tale is too Victorian and heartbreaking to be borne. You have to tell her what really happened. And then maybe there will be a happy ending, after all. I do love happy endings. Almost as much as I love this cake." He groans, his eyelids fluttering." You really should force down a bite or two, teddy bear. It's to die for."

"All right, since you're twisting my arm." I force a smile and take a bite of cake. I don't want to think about happy endings. There's not going to be a happy ending for Adeline and me.

The best we can hope for is something a little less sad and painful.

***

Half an hour later, back in our suite, Eduardo kicks off his shoes, announces himself "pickled and pleased about it," and crawls into bed fully clothed.

He's asleep in seconds.

I turn off the lights and close the door, preparing to make myself at home on the sofa bed and try to write at least a paragraph or two of Stupid Fucking Chapter Fucking Five, when my cell rings. It's a number I don't recognize, but I pick up anyway, willing to talk to a telemarketer if I have to—any excuse to avoid productivity.

"I need advice, man," a familiar voice says before I've had a chance to speak.

"Mitch." I sink onto the sofa with a smile. "Were your ears burning? I was just talking about you."

"Making the Eat, Pray, Jerking Off joke again, you son of a bitch?"

I laugh softly, not wanting to wake Eduardo, who clearly needs to sleep off some of that wine and food. "It's a good joke. And I'm too tired to work up any original material. The new book is killing me. Book length non-fiction is a soul sucker."

"Oh, cry me a fucking river, Mr. Big Book Deal. So you have to write real-life stuff instead of monster stuff. I think you're going to fucking survive."

"Maybe." I sigh. Lately writing has felt like pulling teeth—very healthy, secure, much-loved teeth that don't want to be wrenched from their natural habitat and trapped on paper. "Or maybe I just need to do some more research. All the fieldwork is done, but I could probably do some more expert interviews. More reading. Something."

"Speaking of research," Mitch says, clearing his throat uncomfortably. "I may have pitched a stupid article to *Bait* about women living to please assholes who treat them like shit."

"You've pitched worse." I let my head fall back onto the couch cushion, wishing I had finished my glass of port. I'm still feeling way too wide awake, and I doubt sleep will be happening for me any time soon. "And some women do like assholes who treat them like shit. Take Monty.

He's a complete dick who doesn't shower, and he's practically drowning in pussy."

"Yes! Exactly!" Mitch says, voice rising. "I was thinking of that toe-rot-smelling bastard when I pitched the piece. I was also thinking that I need money to book a flight out of Paris, and *Bait* pays promptly, if not well. But then I started texting some random women on this phone I found, and now I kind of feel like shit."

I frown. "Hold on. A random phone you *found*? Are you calling me from a stolen phone?"

"No, I *found* it. It was sitting on a bench in the park. It must have fallen out of this woman's purse."

"So you just picked it up and started using it?" I ask, incredulous.

"What was I suppose to do." He huffs. "Leave it there and let someone else steal it? Someone who would have tried to get into this girl's bank account and her Facebook page and all the other private stuff I could easily access from this device if I were a bad guy?"

"As opposed to a guy who's just texting her friends and…doing what? Being an asshole to prove a point for a stupid article?"

"Hey, now," he says defensively. "You didn't think it was stupid a few minutes ago. And I'm not hurting anyone. I'm not going to show any of the tit pics I get, I'm just going to mention that I got them."

"You convinced strangers to send you shots of

their breasts by being a dick?" I stand, pacing toward the sliding glass doors leading out onto the balcony. "You've got to be kidding me."

"I only got one actually, and she was ninety and had tits that would scare your balls right off, but that's not the reason I need advice. I'm also texting with this other girl, who seems sweet, but pretty bummed out. She touched a nerve when we first started texting, and I went kind of hard on her. Now I feel shitty about it. So I'm thinking maybe I should apologize and let her know it was just a stunt. That way she knows not everyone in the world is a douchebag. What do you think?"

I snort. "Only you would call me with a problem like this."

"Just give me advice, asshole. This phone could get shut off at any minute. I need to act fast."

"Yes," I say, rolling my eyes. "Apologize, Mitch. Quit being a dick. Ditch this article and pitch something to *Polit-i-spin* instead. Something about the rising terrors of populism and how the world is hurtling toward annihilation or something. That's always an easy sell in these fucked up times."

Mitch sighs, sounding relieved. "Yeah. You're right. This isn't me. I'm a lover, not a douchebag. Okay, one more quick question before I have to go."

"Shoot." I slide open the glass and step out into the frigid night, where the stars are putting on a show unlike anything I've seen in ages. In the city, the glitter on the ground outshines the stars, tricking you into taking all the drama at eye level way too seriously.

"Oh fuck." Mitch shouts something falsely cheery-sounding in French before adding in a whisper, "Gotta run. Catch you later, man."

Before I can tell Mitch to stay out of trouble, the line goes dead.

I slide my phone into my pocket with a shake of my head, sort of wishing Mitch hadn't had to hang up. Nothing like someone else's drama to keep your mind off of your own troubles. Now I'm left alone with the cold air, the dark sky, and the stars that stretch out to infinity, reminding me that I'm a speck of dust, a momentary flash of light on the water—there and gone again in a heartbeat.

Usually I like that about the stars, how small they make me feel. Contemplating my smallness gives me courage. My life will be over in a blink of the great cosmic eye. That means there's no excuse for holding back or giving in or clinging to the lifeboat when it's time to dive into the ocean and swim like hell toward the next adventure.

But not tonight.

Tonight I'm remembering what it felt like to transcend smallness, to feel invincible because I got to love a girl who made every minute of every day feel soaked through with meaning. With purpose. At eighteen, I was so sure that I'd been made to love her—even when I was so confused about everything else.

But now I'm not sure of anything except that I have to do something to make things better with Adeline. Life might be short, but even one blink of the cosmic eye is too long to live with the knowledge that I helped make a good person like Addie so fucking sad.

Chapter ELEVEN

Adeline

Pervert in Paris was wrong about Nate, but maybe he's right about getting out and meeting new people.

I have five contacts on my phone—Shane, Catherine, Penny, Eloise, and the sandwich shop on the corner of 87th where Eloise likes to get Ruebens on Sundays. And I should probably delete Eloise and the sandwich shop, since Eloise is no longer my boss and I've never been a fan of sauerkraut. That takes me down to three contacts, and Cat and Penny are really Shane's friends. Sure, they're sweet to me when I manage to sneak away for book club or coffee, but if Shane were to drift out of my life, the other girls would follow.

So when morning dawns bright and sunny, and the snow is sparkling like sugar on the slopes outside my window, I decide against staying inside hiding out from Nate and the world.

I've done enough hiding. It's time to get out and live, and maybe make some new friends while I'm at it. There's at least one group of girlfriends here for the Valentine's Day weekend. I saw them checking in yesterday. Maybe I can convince them to take pity on me and let me join them for girls-only V-day dinner tomorrow night.

I wasn't always an anti-social hermit, after all. There was a time when I had lots of girlfriends, an entire crew of fellow book nerds and band nerds and drama geeks who understood my love of good stories and tolerated my enthusiasm for math.

I can learn to be that person again.

"Not every relationship has to end badly," I say to my reflection as I finish wrestling my hair into braids and push my glasses up my nose. "Just because your mom and dad and brothers and extended family and Nate and Eloise all decided they would be just fine with you dropping off the face of the earth into a pit that has no end, that doesn't mean the rest of the world is anti-Adeline."

For a second, I almost start laughing hysterically—again with the laugh or cry! Ba-dum-dum—but instead I tug on my new red knit cap with the fluffy pom-pom on the top and march determinedly out the door.

Early this morning, long before the rest of the

lodge was stirring, I'd dropped four hundred dollars I couldn't afford to spend in the ski shop downstairs. But thanks to a killer end of season sale, I managed to score a pair of red ski pants, a base layer shirt, an ultra-insulated, water-repellent black hoodie, my spiffy new hat, and an outfit to wear around the lodge, which I'll be able to swap out with my sweater dress.

It has warmed up to just above freezing so I should be fine to head out for an hour or two without my wool coat, which won't fair well if I end up getting tossed off my sled into a snow bank. I haven't sledded since I was maybe ten years old, and I'm not sure I'll remember how, but I'm still excited.

The day is truly gorgeous. The air is clean and sweet as I step out of the lodge and start up the trail to the sledding hill, and there's no sign of Nate or his very nice boyfriend. As I walk, it occurs to me that Eduardo seemed to like me just fine—he certainly had no trouble chatting with me non-stop on the way up to the lodge yesterday—and would probably make a good friend.

But I can't be friends with someone who's dating Nate. Like it or not, there are still feelings there. Feelings and longings and an aversion to being close to someone who is in love with Nate and has an intimate relationship with the only penis I've ever touched.

So I mark Eduardo off my potential friends list

and get in line for a sled. The equipment manager sets me up with a shiny silver disc with handles on either side, a helmet I decide not to wear because it won't fit over my hat, and a scarf he says someone left a few weeks ago that I can have free of charge.

"Thank you so much," I say, grinning as I wrap the cozy black fleece around my neck.

"No problem." The manager returns my smile, his blue eyes crinkling at the edges as he tucks his long blond hair behind his ears. "Glad it fits. Let me know if you need anything else, okay? Anything at all. I'm Chase, and I'm here until noon."

"Adeline, and thank you. Will do." I wave and turn to go, my sled clutched in one hand, wondering if Chase was flirting with me. I glance back over my shoulder to find him watching me go, and wave again, feeling a little fizzy when he waves back and his grin goes goofy on one side.

He *was* flirting with me!

And he's cute, in a surfer dude who got lost on a ski slope kind of way. And he seems nice and generous with the Lost and Found stash!

I'm considering doing something crazy (for me) like going back to the shed a few minutes before noon and asking Chase if he would like to get coffee, when I reach the turn off to the sledding hill to find Nate leaning against a tree near the trail. Immediately, my heart starts pounding the way it does every time I lay eyes on the man. He's wearing what looks like a cross between a motorcycle jacket and a ski coat, gray ski pants, black boots, and reflective glasses, and looks hot enough to catch the snow on fire.

He belongs on the cover of *Snobby European Skiing, Sex God Edition.* His silky brown hair is tousled, and his unshaven morning stubble makes his mouth look even more sexy and dangerous. He lifts a hand and smiles in greeting, and my stomach does a swooping back flip, reminding me that normal men might make me fizz, but only this pretty devil has ever knocked me off my feet.

The bastard. I am ruined for other men, and it's all his gorgeous fault.

I scowl at him, preparing to storm past without saying a word, but he steps into the path, blocking my way.

"Please, Addie." He shifts his glasses to the top of his head, pinning me with that infuriating soulful gaze of his. "Five minutes. Give me five minutes, and then if you decide you still hate my guts and want nothing to do with me, I'll leave you alone. I promise. Cross my heart and hope to die."

I bite my lip, teeth digging in deep. I don't want to give him five minutes, but it would be unreasonable to refuse.

And I am reasonable, logical Adeline Klein, who always does her best to be polite and friendly and put other people at ease, even when other people are being huge jerks. I have spent my entire adult life bending over backward for a tyrant boss who treated me like an unwanted orphan from a gothic novel and will probably spend the next however many years bending over backward for cranky New Yorkers while I'm serving coffee or schlepping drinks or cleaning toilets or whatever job I can get with no references, no resume, and very little experience.

But right now, I'm on a vacation, damn it. My first vacation since I was a kid going camping with this asshole, and I'm not in the mood to be reasonable.

Screw reasonable.

And screw Nate Casey.

"No." I smile as I bounce lightly on my toes. "You can not have five minutes. And your promises mean nothing to me. Less than nothing, in fact. So take your promises and your stupid sexy face and go eat about a pound of rotten eggs!"

Before he can reply, I dash past him, boots crunching in the lightly packed snow.

I don't stop at the top of the hill. I keep going, getting a running start before tossing my sled onto the snow and jumping onto the disc. And for a few moments, everything is amazing.

I'm zipping away from Nate, who has no sled—ha, ha! Take that, P.D.!—making my triumphant escape down the hill toward the lodge. But just as I'm starting to enjoy the zing of the cool breeze on my face, I hit something hard hidden under the snow and my disc spins in a dizzy half circle.

Suddenly I'm hurtling down the hill backward, which is not nearly as much fun as being able to see where I'm going and know that I'm not going to ram into a tree and kill myself. I lean into the spin, hoping to take myself the rest of the way around, but instead, my shiny silver disc veers wildly across the slope, into the path of oncoming sleds.

I scream, holding a hand out in front of me, as if that will somehow magically keep me from a head on collision. I avoid getting slammed by a man three times my size on a steerable sled, who jerks his Flexible Flyer off course in time to miss me, but I hit a tube full of kids, sending tiny pink and orange-coated bodies bouncing into the air as my sled careens into the trees.

Faster, faster, I zip through the shadows, past tree trunks and over more bumpy things hidden beneath the snow as thin branches slap at my back and shoulders, but do nothing to slow my slide. I'm guessing I'm travelling at something close to the speed of light, so fast I'm afraid to stick out an arm or leg for fear that it will be snapped off and I'll continue my plunge down the mountain with a bleeping stump where a limb used to be.

I'm praying for a snow bank, or maybe a rotted tree—surely colliding with a rotten tree will hurt less than hitting a healthy one—when the ground suddenly disappears beneath me. I gasp, my heart lurching into my throat as I look down, realizing there's a good fifteen-foot drop to the snow below me. The sled hangs tauntingly in the air long enough for me to get psychotically scared before falling hard and fast toward what I hope will be a drift deep enough to break my fall.

Seconds later, I land flat on my back with an *oof* that's echoed by the sled as it slaps down a few feet away and shivers across the snow to spin in a lazy circle near a very large rock. I'm staring at the rock, thinking about how much worse things would be right now if I'd fallen on it instead of the snow, and silently thanking the gods of sledding that I'm alive, when I hear a male voice shout—

"Fuck! Shit! Shit!"

—from somewhere overhead.

A moment later a steerable sled shoots off the ledge, soaring over my head to ram into a tree, splintering to pieces.

I flinch and cough, the breath rushing back into my lungs. I'm trying to roll over, figuring I'd better get up before my luck runs out and someone lands on top of me, when Nate's head pops up above the snow bank. "Adeline! Are you okay? Are you hurt?"

My eyes narrow. "You."

"Stay there, I'll be right down," he says, clearly not realizing that he's the last person I want to see while I'm lying in the snow in a defeated heap.

"I don't need help," I call out, but I don't try to get up again. I've already embarrassed myself enough in front of Nate. I refuse to give him the satisfaction of seeing me wallow around in a snowdrift like an artic walrus.

In what feels like no time, he's found his way down to the scene of my humiliation and fallen to his knees beside me. "Just lie still." The concern on his face as he tugs off his gloves is almost funny. Too bad I'm not in the mood to laugh anymore. "I have first aid training. Not a lot, but enough to see if anything's broken. Can you tell me where it hurts?"

"It doesn't hurt," I insist, still making no move to rise. "I'm fine. You can leave."

He scowls, and his eyes flash the way they do when he's angry. Or turned on. Or maybe angrily turned on, though I've never personally seen him in that state. "You just sledded off a goddamned ledge, Adeline," he says, voice rough. "And you're not moving."

"I don't feel like moving," I say stubbornly. "I'm enjoying a rest in the snow. So go away, Nate. Go, go, go away, and don't come back another day."

His breath rushes out. "That's mature."

"Yeah? Well, screw mature," I say, the heat in my tone surprising me. "I did mature. I did all the mature while you were off hitting keg parties. I don't have to do mature right now, and I don't have to talk to you. So go away!"

Nate's jaw clenches and I'm pretty sure he's about to lose his temper in a fashion unlike anything I've seen from him before.

Instead he leans in, wrapping his hands around my wrists, pinning them to the snow. "I'm not going away," he whispers inches from my lips, making my pulse spike. "Not until you let me get through to you, one way or another."

"If you kiss me, I'm going to bite you," I warn, heart racing.

"Fine by me. I like it when you bite." And then he kisses me. He kisses me hard and deep and my stupid body lights up like a California brush fire.

My nerve endings ignite, and fireworks launch behind my closed eyes, and I moan into his mouth like he's the best thing that's ever happened to my lips. And he is, the bastard. He tastes so good, so incredibly good, like the first drink of water after hours spent boiling in the summer heat—fresh and clean and explosively delicious.

His tongue lays claim to my mouth and I feel it everywhere, in every secret place that's been dark and shadowed since he went away. The kiss rips through me, pulling the curtains from the walls, throwing open windows, letting the sun shine in, leaving me no place to hide from the knowledge that I have missed his kisses like I would miss air. Like I would miss books and music and art and waking up every morning knowing there are still more beautiful things in the world left to discover.

But none of them are as beautiful as Nate's lips on mine or his groan as I nip his bottom lip or the way his thigh presses between my legs as he shifts on top of me.

He kisses me, and the years melt away, and suddenly I'm sixteen, young and fearless and drunk on my first taste of how wonderful it is to get this close to someone. So close that his breath is my breath and his heart is my heart and his hunger is all the food I'll ever need.

"You feel so good, Ad." He drops a hand to my hip, gripping me tight through my ski pants. "It was always so fucking good with you."

"I still want you," I confess, as the fingers of my newly freed hand find their way up the back of his coat. "I want to touch you everywhere."

"If we wouldn't die of exposure, I would take you right now." His hand moves between my legs. Even through the thick fabric, his touch feels insanely amazing, making me moan and arch into his mouth as he kisses his way down my throat. "I would take you here in the snow and prove that I still remember exactly how to make you come for me, Einstein."

I wince, the old pet name sending pain flashing through my pleasure. "Less talk, more kissing," I say, trying to guide his mouth back to mine.

"Talk first." His hand returns to my hip,

robbing me of the sweet, teasing pressure of his fingers between my legs. "And then we're going inside, where I can get you out of at least some of these clothes."

"Not going to happen," I say, knowing myself better than that. "I'm not thinking straight right now, but I will be soon, and then I'm going to tell you to get your hands off of me."

"Maybe." Sadness flickers behind his eyes. "But at least you'll know the truth."

"And what is the truth, Nate?" My blood is still so hot I can barely feel the snow creeping through my hair to prick at the bare skin above my new scarf. "That you really are a devil crawled out of a New Jersey hellmouth?"

He sighs, his jaw working back and forth the way it always did when he was getting ready to say something he knows I won't want to hear. "While we were up here on our trip, my father found the paperwork I was going to file to transfer to Rutgers. He got on my laptop, emptied my checking account, and went through all my private shit, looking for something he could use to make me see things his way. He found it in my Dropbox. I had my phone set to automatically back up all the images. Before I even got home, he'd already downloaded the pictures from the lake and figured out who you were...and how old you *weren't*."

"What pictures from the lake?" My eyes widen as my mind coughs up the memory. "Oh my

God. The topless pictures?"

Nate grimaces. "Yeah. Those. I don't know if you remember, but my dad was a lawyer. *Is* a lawyer. He helpfully informed me that possession of those pictures was a crime. It didn't matter if you'd willingly posed for them or not. You were under eighteen, and I was technically an adult, so…"

"Oh my God," I say again, too shocked to think of anything more eloquent.

"He told me to pack my things and get ready to go to Duke that afternoon." Nate's voice is tight. "I had to leave without telling you good-bye and agree never to talk to you again or he'd have me prosecuted for possessing child pornography."

My jaw falls and my blood goes cold.

Ice cold—the temperature of Nate's father's arctic heart.

Chapter TWELVE

Nate

I wait for Addie to say something, anything, but she just stares up at the sky, looking shell-shocked.

I'm still laying half on top of her in the snow, and I know I should get up. I should make her stand, too, even if she decides my explanation doesn't change the way she feels. It's cold and, as the sun slips behind the clouds, getting colder. But it feels so fucking good to be this close to her, so close that I can feel her breath warm on my lips and smell her Adeline smell—flowers and fresh rain—rising all around me.

"Did you hear me, Ad?" I finally ask.

She nods, gaze still fixed over my shoulder.

"He said there was a chance I would be charged with intent to distribute," I say, needing her to understand why I'd been so spooked. "If convicted, I would have served a minimum of five years in prison and been required to register as a sex offender for the rest of my life."

Addie shakes her head slowly, but still doesn't meet my gaze.

I let my eyes drift to her lips, those bow-shaped lips that are every bit as sweet and irresistible as they were seven years ago, but I don't kiss her again. I shouldn't have kissed her the first time, but I didn't know how else to get through to her. And she's so sexy when she's angry, with her eyes on fire and her skin flushed pink.

"So that's why you left," she finally says, her voice soft, distant.

"It doesn't excuse it, I know that. I shouldn't have left. Or at the very least I should have called to explain, but my dad was watching me like a fucking hawk. He said the second I tried to contact you he would call his friend at the police department." I sigh. "But finally, about halfway through October, I pulled my head out of my ass and realized I had to fight back, even if it meant risking going to jail. I dropped out of school and drove straight to your house, but you were gone."

"I was gone," Addie agrees, brow furrowing. "It looks like it's going to rain. Or maybe snow. It feels colder than it did when I came out."

I press my lips together, nodding slowly. "Is that all you have to say? If so, that's fine, I just..." I trail off with a miserable shrug. "I just wanted you to know the truth. I didn't want to leave. I was scared away, but I came back. I swear I did. I'm sorry it was too late, and that you had to wait so long to hear the truth."

Pained resignation flashes in her pretty blue eyes, so sad behind her glasses. "Well, I guess it doesn't matter now, does it?"

"It matters to me." Regret spreads like a virus through my chest, making it hard to breathe. She was right. I'm not going to be taking Addie back inside and getting her out of any of these clothes. I may never kiss her again, and though I knew that was always a possibility, now that I've tasted her, felt her, heard her sexy little moan as I pressed my hand between her legs, the thought of going without Adeline forever makes me feel like something vital is shutting down inside of me.

"It matters a lot," I continue, voice tight. "I loved you, Adeline."

"I loved you, too." She lifts a gloved hand, pressing it lightly to my cheek. "You were the best thing that ever happened to me. Right up until you were the worst."

Well, *fuck*…

Fuck me. Fuck me for hurting her even more than I thought I did. Fuck me for secretly assuming that I'd loved her more than she'd loved me, and that running away and leaving me with no way to reach her had been easy for her. Fuck me for giving up and moving on and telling myself pretty lies that everything had worked out for the best.

Everything hasn't worked out for the best. Adeline, girl genius, pint-sized powerhouse, with the biggest heart I've ever known, is lying beneath me, shattered and sad and, worst of all, *resigned* to it. And I played a role in her despair.

"I don't... I just..." I trail off, words failing me for the first time in years. I'm a writer by trade; I traffic in turns of phrase, but none of my words are good enough. I'm standing at the edge of the abyss, and Addie's already falling. There's no time to waste. I need the perfect words, the perfect rope to throw down into the darkness.

I wrack my brain, thinking of the stars last night, and smallness, and how good it felt to belong to someone. To belong to this woman, to Adeline of the nimble mind and the good heart and the beautiful body that gave me more than pleasure. It gave me hope and home and strength.

I'm thinking about a quote by Carl Sagan about the universe and love, one that always makes me think of that perfect summer, but before I can remember it, the rumble of an engine fills the air.

Seconds later, a guy with long blond hair pulls a snowmobile to a stop a few feet away and hops out onto the ground. He's got a good-natured face, but there's a hard look in his eyes as he asks, "Are you okay, Adeline? I saw your sled head into the trees and came as fast as I could."

I roll away, coming to my feet as Addie sits up.

"Yes, thank you, I'm fine. The only thing wounded is my pride." She ignores the hand I offer to help her up, struggling to her feet on her own. "Chase, this is my old friend Nate. Nate, this is Chase, the very nice equipment manager who gave me this toasty scarf." She brushes her hair from her face. "My neck is still mostly warm, though the rest of me isn't sure leaving my coat in the room was the best idea."

As if on cue, the clouds above us shake out a flurry of flakes that drift down to settle like lace on Addie's dark curls. She glances up with a sigh, avoiding eye contact with me like it's her job.

Chase, however, has no issues with glaring at me like it's his.

"Let me give you a ride back to the lodge," he says, holding a hand out to Addie. "I'll come back and get your sled later."

"Thank you," Adeline says. "That would be great. Is there room for Nate, too?"

"Sorry, afraid not," Chase says, not sounding sorry at all. "But I can come back for you, sir. If you need help getting back to the lodge."

"No, I'm fine. I can walk." I meet his cool gaze as Addie crosses to the snowmobile. "But be careful with her. She's one of the best people I know."

Addie's eyes shift my way, surprise and caution mixing in her gaze. But before I can tell her that I mean it, or that I still have so many things I need to say to her, Chase sets the snowmobile to roaring. He guides the vehicle through the trees toward the lodge, taking Adeline away again.

But as they're about to disappear into the trees, Addie turns and looks back at me. She looks back, and then she's gone.

But not for forever this time.

Our paths are going to cross again. I'm going to make damned sure of it.

Chapter THIRTEEN

Adeline

Back at my room, I discover a blinking light on my phone and the following messages from my nearest and fearest.

Voice message from Shane: Hey darling! I'm so sorry for the mess with my cell. And I hate that a French creeper was texting you obscene things!

Of all the creepers I've known, French creepers are some of the worst. Remind me to tell you a disturbing story about a Parisian man in my pre-med program and a wheel of Brie when I get home.

Anyway! I hope you're all right and back to enjoying yourself. I would have called your cell, but my pregnant brain couldn't remember your number. I've become so dependent on my contact list I barely have my own phone number memorized anymore.

All is great here. Jake and I are having a lovely time, and Paris is beautiful, even in the winter. I'm planning to bring back a carry-on bag full of pastries, and we'll gorge ourselves on croissants, drink too much tea, and plot the next step in your adventure as soon as I get home. I'm so glad you dumped Eloise, and I still very much hope you'll give me the opportunity to help you get back on your feet. It would truly be my pleasure.

Okay, talk soon, doll. Hope you're having fun! I'm going to put off getting a new cell until Jake and I get back to the city, but feel free to call me at the hotel if you need anything at all.

Or on Jake's cell. His number is…

She leaves the number, which I write down, though I have no intention of calling and interrupting her romantic getaway again, no matter how desperately I need to talk to someone about Nate.

About Nate and his confession and that kiss that turned my world upside down.

My fingers drift to my lips, brushing lightly across the skin, thinking of his taste and his touch and how much I want more of both as I wait for the second message to start.

This time, however, the voice on the line is significantly less friendly.

Voicemail from Eloise: Hello, Adeline, this is Eloise. Don't ask me how I found you. You know I have my ways, and that when I want something I get it.

Not that you'll care, but earlier today, while on my way to the park with Mina, I was accosted by that homeless deviant you love so much. He expectorated on my shoes, Adeline. Right on the patent leather of my Maison Margeilas! And for once—despite having at least four more children than any decent person should have—Mina didn't have baby wipes in her purse. I was forced to leave the diseased evidence of his contempt for decency on my shoe until we made it back to the house. It was a violation of my dignity from which I doubt I'll ever completely recover.

As things stand now, I doubt I'll leave our building again, at least not without an armed guard or a police escort.

And the saddest part of all, of course, is that this tragedy was avoidable. If you had respected my concerns, this wouldn't have happened, Adeline! I blame you every bit as much as that heathen whom you encouraged with your attentions.

Therefore, I will be withholding your final check.

It only seems fair considering *you're* the one who quit without giving two weeks' notice. Poor Mina has had to work extended hours to escort me to my appointments, and I have no idea what's going on in the world now that's there's no one here to read the *Times*. If I can't find a decent replacement for you soon, I will be reduced to watching CNN like a troglodyte.

I hope you're enjoying your little escape from reality. Just remember that the piper always comes calling, and nothing in this world is free. One day Shane is going to call in all the favors she's done for you, little miss, and I have a feeling you're not going to like the price you'll be expected to pay.

No one's as nice as she pretends to be, girl. She wants something, and I imagine it's something pretty foul if she's willing to spend thousands of dollars buttering you up with fancy vacations to get it.

Enjoy selling your soul to the devil, and don't come crying to me when you find yourself out on the street a second time.

"Oh, for Christ's sake, Eloise," I mutter, slamming the phone back into the cradle a little too hard.

Shane isn't the devil, and poor Kevin isn't a "deviant." I'm guessing the entire thing was an accident. He was probably spitting and Eloise's shoe just happened to be in the way. And even if he meant to spit on her, she deserves it for the way she curled her lip at him every time we passed by, not to mention her plan to have him arrested for crimes he didn't commit.

The woman is unhinged.

She's also obscenely wealthy. My check is barely a blip on her monthly expense sheet—she spends more money on exotic groceries and collectible stamps—but that won't stop her from refusing to pay me.

Which means I'm fifteen hundred dollars poorer than I expected to be.

I flop down onto the bed with a groan, my arms spread wide and my head spinning. I should be thinking about what I'm going to do for money and whether or not to move to a cheaper city while I still have the funds to get out New York. I should be figuring out what I want to study and charting my course for a return to academia, where I always felt safe and at home.

And if I am incapable of thinking ahead due to the stress of quitting the only job I've ever had, learning the only man I've ever loved is gay, and then learning that he isn't gay—or at least not open and shut gay because we totally almost had snow sex—then I should have accepted Chase's offer to grab hot chocolate and warm up by the fire. It's been years since I've been asked on anything resembling a date, but instead of jumping at the chance to enjoy a sugary drink with a perfectly nice man with highlights in his unicorn-mane-like hair, I'm lying here thinking about Nate.

About Nate and the way he pinned my arms to the ground and that kiss that rocked me to the core of my being. Of his hand between my legs, awakening a hunger I hadn't thought I was capable of feeling anymore. I had assumed that my capacity for rampant, wildfire-devouring-the-prairie kind of lust had been snuffed out years ago.

I haven't even felt run-of-the-mill sexual interest in months. That little fizz when Chase waved at me was the most action my hormones have gotten since a sexy Wall Street type winked at me while I was walking in the park with Shane. And he could have just had something in his eye. Or been winking at Shane. She's a stunning beauty with excellent taste in clothing, naturally blond hair, and spectacular boobs. I'm more the fuzzy-haired sidekick type, like Hermione Granger before she turned gorgeous, or that little critter that lives in Jabba the Hutt's fat folds.

"Not when you're with him," I mutter to the paint swirls on the ceiling. When I'm with Nate, I don't feel like a fat fold creature. I feel like a five-alarm sex goddess. I feel beautiful and desirable and...enough. More than enough.

But what I really am, I suddenly realize, is a cheater.

I bolt upright, hair flying into my face. "Eduardo!"

Oh my God! How could I have forgotten about Eduardo! Sweet Eduardo, who so generously offered his help and comfort to me, the very woman who became his boyfriend's cheating accomplice less than twenty-four hours later!

Where the hell does Nate get off? How does he think it's okay to stalk me and kiss me and talk feelings, when he's here with his significant other?!

"Because he's a liar and you know it, Adeline!" I shout to the empty room as I rip off my ski clothes and fetch my sweater dress from the closet, secretly relieved to have a reason to be mad at Nate again.

For about an hour there, I wasn't sure what to feel other than sad, stunned, and desperate to kiss him again.

If his story is true, then I can't blame him for being scared. Realizing his dad was a monster who would rather see his son go to prison than allow him to live his own life couldn't have been easy. And then there was the look in Nate's eyes when he said that he'd loved me—that intense, searing, melting look that made me want to believe that our summer of love wasn't a lie, after all.

But now I remember Eduardo. Innocent, gullible Eduardo who has been sucked in by Nate's sex vibe and fallen prey to the same lying devil who took a jackhammer to my heart years ago. Nate is a heartbreaker, a *life* breaker, and the last person Ed should be thinking about adopting puppies with.

Sparing a few minutes to unbraid my hair,

smooth frizz cream through my curls, and slap on a coat of lipstick for confidence, I slam out of my room on a mission of mercy. I'm not sure where I'll find Eduardo, but I will scour every inch of this property if I have to. I will find him, confess my sins, and beg him to break up with Nate before it's too late. Before he's in so deep that he'll never be able to get Nathaniel Casey out of his dirty dreams.

I've been having sex dreams about Nate for over seven years. Seven flipping years! Nearly a fourth of my entire life, and who knows when or if my subconscious will give it up.

The realization makes me even madder. I storm down the wide staircase leading to the lobby, boots thudding on the carpet. I glare at the Valentine's Day Tree, where hearts and flowers and explosions of pink and red sparkly string hang from the bare limbs of an artificial ash. Whoever bastardized this Christmas holiday tradition should be dragged out into the wilderness and made to live on acorns and melted snow. Or at the very least forced to wear a sweater made of sparkly string and walk around the lodge looking like a puddle of unicorn vomit until the poor tree is put out of its misery.

I circle the monstrosity, contempt curling my upper lip—love is a lie, and love with sparkles on it is just a lie bedazzled—and head across the lobby toward the restaurant. It's nearly lunchtime. If I'm lucky, maybe I'll catch Eduardo getting ready to eat and be able to pull him aside for a private chat.

I'm mentally composing what I'm going to say to poor Ed, knowing I can't afford to downplay the intensity of the kiss I shared with Nate—or leave out the part where Nate announced his intention to take me inside and get me out of my clothes—when the devil himself pushes through the doors on the east side of the lobby.

Nate is still wearing his ski clothes, and his tousled hair is covered with fat snowflakes. Apparently he's just found his way back to the lodge through the storm that's swirling thicker and faster around the hotel than it was when Chase dropped me off nearly an hour ago. He looks cold, gorgeous, and determined, and there's no doubt that he's spotted me, too. The second he steps through the doors, his eyes lock on mine, sending prickles of awareness stabbing at me like tiny darts, threatening to let all the air out of my anger balloon.

I freeze, hands curling into fists at my side as he starts my way with long, sure strides. I hold my ground, eyes narrowing as I prepare for confrontation.

I refuse to be talked out of telling Eduardo everything. He deserves to know the truth. Ignorance is not bliss. I learned that the hard way, when I spent months waiting for Nate to find me, only to wake up every day alone, with no way back to the happy, carefree girl I was before

Hurricane Nathaniel swept through my life.

But I'm not going to let that happen to someone else, not if I can prevent it.

"We're not done," Nate says in a deep, sexy voice that makes my lips tingle and my sweater dress suddenly feel too hot.

"We are completely done." I ignore my traitorous body, which clearly has no idea what's best for it. "But Eduardo and I have a few things to talk about."

He frowns, seemingly genuinely confused, the bastard.

Has he no shame at all? Absolutely none?

"He seems like a really nice man," I push on, blood beginning to boil. "Who deserves better than a boyfriend who will cheat on him and clearly feel no guilt about it whatsoever. You really are a piece of work, Casey, and I can't believe I forgot that for even a fraction of a fraction of a second!"

The tension melts from Nate's handsome face and the jerk actually has the nerve to smile. "Shit. I can't believe I forgot about that part. I was just—"

"You forgot about *that* part?" I squeak, volume rising sharply as my outrage approaches critical mass. "About what part? The part where you kissed me or the part where you have a boyfriend whose heart you're going to break?"

"Lower your voice," his says, casting a wary look over my shoulder. "We can't do this here.

Let's go somewhere private to talk, okay?"

"Go somewhere private so you won't be embarrassed by an ugly public confrontation about what a dirty rotten cheater you are? No, Nate. Sorry, but I don't care if I'm making a scene. I don't care if everyone in this lodge hears that—"

My words end in a yip of surprise as Nate wraps an arm around my waist, spins us both in a half circle, and starts back toward the doors leading outside.

"Stop it! Let me go!" I dig my heels into the carpet, but Nate only tightens his grip, lifting me off the ground and carrying me the last few steps to the doors.

Before I can recover from the indignity of being hauled out of the lobby like a sack of potatoes, we're outside and a blast of artic air takes my breath away.

"I don't have my coat on," I gasp, shivering as the wind cuts through the fabric of my dress, immediately making my skin go numb. "Wh-what are you trying to do? Freeze me to death before I can get to Eduardo?"

"I'm making sure you don't ruin something I know you won't want to ruin once you understand what's going on." He hauls me around a stone pillar and along the sidewalk leading to the far side of the lodge. "And we'll be back inside soon. If I put you down, will you walk with me? Give me a chance to explain?"

"Yes. Let me walk." The second my feet touch the ground, I dash back toward the lodge, but I barely make it three steps before Nate's arms are around me again.

"All right. Then we'll do this the hard way," he says, flipping me over his shoulder.

As my bottom goes up and my head falls forward, nearly sending my glasses flying, I cry out in outrage, but there's no one around to hear me. We're out of sight of the uniformed staff manning the main lobby doors, and everyone else has retreated to the lodge in the face of the increasingly ugly storm. There's no one around to object to this clear violation of my free will, or to appreciate the sharp *smack* of the flat of my hand on Nate's ass.

"Put me down!" I slap him again, trying not to think about how firm and delicious his ass is or how much I once enjoyed digging my fingers into it as he made love to me.

"I'm sorry, I can't," he says. "You can hit me as much as you want, but I'm not letting you go until we talk it all out. No more distractions."

I bring both hands down on his bottom, sending a sting across my bare palms as I begin to shiver. "This is ki-kidnapping. You can't do this!"

"I'm not kidnapping you, Addie. I'm taking you to my room so we can talk. Alone. Without anyone around to interrupt or overhear or give you an excuse to run off and do the hokey-pokey. And when we're finished, if you want to leave, I'll let you go. I promise."

I huff. "You already know what I think of your promises."

"I do," he says, "but I'm going to change your mind. I'm not the monster you think I am, Einstein. And I care about you too much to let you walk away from me without knowing that you deserve good things and someone who will do whatever it takes to make you happy."

The anger chugging away inside of me loses steam. I remind myself that Nate is a liar, but he sounds so sincere. He sounds like he means every word, and I can't help wondering what it would be like to believe in him again. To believe that he cares about me, and that he's out there somewhere in the world wishing me well instead of busy forgetting the name of the girl he slept with the summer before college.

Would it make it easier to move on, or harder?

I don't know, but I find I no longer feel like slapping him repeatedly.

I settle in for the ride to wherever Nate is taking me, trying not to admire the view too much. Yes, Nate is beautiful, and his backside is the loveliest backside I've ever seen, but he's taken. Besides, friendship would never work between us, let alone anything more.

No matter how much I want him, we will never be together again. It's as impossible as rolling back the tide or sending all the snowflakes pelting my face swirling back where they came from.

Chapter FOURTEEN

Nate

E duardo will be at the spa until two.

That means I have approximately two hours to prove to Adeline that I'm not a cheating, lying bastard. And that I'm also not gay, which I would prefer to do with something more convincing than words. But if Addie won't kiss me again today, then I'll wait.

I'll wait as long as I have to, and do whatever it takes to prove to her that this thing between us is worth another shot.

Somewhere between the mountain and the lodge it hit me that Addie's eyes aren't the only ones that have lost their light. I've spent years travelling the world, hunting down adventure with a single-minded focus that would make my obsessive-compulsive father proud—if I still talked to the son of a bitch—but I can't remember the last time I felt this alive. Kissing Addie in the snow, feeling her warm and responsive beneath my mouth, has planted a seed of hope inside of me, a magic seed that's already surged into the sky like Jack's beanstalk, making previously crazy ideas seem possible.

Why should Addie and I be defined by a past we were too young to shape? By the actions of a man who cared more about his son playing football than the happiness of two people who loved each other?

Fuck the past. Fuck making amends and moving on. I don't want to move on, not without seeing what Addie and I could be together now that we've both grown up and taken control of our lives. It still feels meant to be. When I touch her all the cynical bullshit I've carried around for years melts away and I realize I wasn't such a dumb kid, after all. At eighteen, I was smart enough to recognize a love worth rewriting the script for when I found it. Now, at twenty-five, I'm old enough to realize that what I feel with Addie might really be a once-in-a-lifetime thing.

I'm not going to give up on her again, not without a fight. Because I know she feels it, too—this connection, the way it's so right to be together again.

I make it through the back entrance to the Raven Wing and into the elevator without being observed. But on the sixth floor, the doors open to reveal an older couple in matching red sweaters.

As I step out of the elevator with Addie still tossed over my shoulder, the woman's eyes widen and her husband's mouth puckers. I smile and offer a cheery "Happy Valentine's Day" before moving away down the hall, knowing from experience that pretending weird shit is normal is enough to put most people at ease.

Thankfully, Adeline doesn't cry out for help, making me hope she's coming around to the idea of talking this through.

But when I set her on her feet inside my room, her expression is still guarded.

"Hey," I say, breath rushing out. "Um, would you like something to drink? Water or coffee or—"

"You wanted to talk." She crosses her arms at her chest. "So talk. But no lies. If you lie, I'm leaving. I want the whole truth and nothing but the truth."

"I can't give you the whole truth," I say, moving to block her path when she tries to dart around me to the door. "I seriously can't, Addie. I signed a non-disclosure agreement."

She pauses, studying me out of the corners of her eyes. "A non-disclosure agreement?"

"Yes. So I can't *legally* tell you why I'm here with Eduardo, but I can tell you that it's not what it seems. I'm not gay, and we're not really together. We're just pretending we are for a good cause."

"Oh my God." Her shoulders slump a moment before her face falls into her hands. "Shit. I'm an idiot."

"You're not an idiot. There's no way you could have known."

"Yes, there is." She looks up, her arms flopping at her sides. "I know about Magnificent Bastard Consulting, Nate. I know that you work for Bash."

I blink. "What?"

"I'm friends with Shane, who is friends with Penny and Cat, Aidan's wife," she says, blowing my mind. What are the chances that she's one of the six or seven people Bash said were in on his secret? Addie, out of all the millions of people in New York City?

"I saw you in the park when you were training with Aidan," she continues. "So I should have at least considered that Eduardo could be your client. I was just so surprised, and it seemed like you two were really in love. Or at least Eduardo seemed like he was in love with *you*." She paces deeper into the room, twirling a lock of hair around her finger the way she does when she's thinking. "You seemed uncomfortable, obviously. But I thought that was because of the way things ended, and seeing each other for the first time, and the fact that you were gay and I was finding out that you were gay. And the implications that had on the past and blah, blah, blah…"

She sits down hard on the couch in front of

the sliding doors, shaking her head listlessly. "But it's just an intervention."

"It's just an intervention," I confirm, figuring it's okay to bend the rules of my non-disclosure agreement since Adeline already knows that I work for MBC. She saw me with Aiden, which means… "So you've known I was in New York for a while?"

"A few months. But only Shane knows that you and I…." Her gaze drifts my way before returning to the coffee table. "That I used to know you. I asked her not to tell Bash or anyone else. I didn't want it to get back to you that I was in the city."

My chest goes tight. "Because you hated me?"

"Because I didn't see any reason to make contact. I didn't know there was anything more to the story," she says, granting me a sliver of hope that another shot with her isn't completely out of the question.

I lean against the bureau, studying her face. "So Shane doesn't know that I told you I was transferring schools to be with you, and then bailed the next day?"

"No," Addie says softly. "She just knows that it didn't end well. I didn't tell her the whole story. I haven't told anyone. I don't… I don't talk about it."

"I'm sorry." I wish I could pull her into my arms and hold her until all the ugliness is gone. "If there's one thing I could go back and change in my entire life it would be leaving the way I did. I swear that's the truth."

"Your father was threatening to send you to prison." She studies her hands, tapping her index fingers and thumbs lightly together. "I understand why you were scared, and why you left. I even understand why it took you a while to come back."

"A little over a month, but your mom said you'd been gone for weeks. I guess you left town not long after I did?"

Adeline looks up, sharp and focused. "You talked to my mom? What did she say?"

"She said that you regretted being with me, and that you'd left to get a fresh start. She also said that I was a monster, that you never wanted to see me again, and that she was going to call the police if I didn't get off her property. I tried to explain, to apologize—but she slammed the door in my face."

A bitter smile curves Addie's lips. "I sent Mom a Christmas card a couple of years after I left home. I thought I should try to mend fences, no matter how much it hurt, and she'd always loved Christmas." She shrugs. "She sent it back unopened. That was the last time I tried to contact her or anyone else in my family. I haven't even seen the boys. But they were so young when I left home they probably don't even remember me that much."

I curse beneath my breath. "What the hell

happened, Adeline?"

"I had sex before marriage and Mom found out about it," she says, with a tired roll of her eyes. "So I had to leave before I could infect any of my little brothers with my propensity for sin."

My brow furrows tight. "That's insane. What the hell is wrong with her? Your parents always sounded so nice. At least compared to my dad."

"I'm sure they're still nice. As long as you don't break any of the rules. My mom is really good at remembering the rules. She's not so great at remembering those Bible stories about forgiveness and mercy and welcoming home the prodigal son. Or daughter, in my case."

"And your dad?" I ask, getting progressively sick to my stomach.

"Same." Her eyes close for a long beat before they open again. "No, not the same, but he does what Mom tells him to do. He values peace in his home more than a relationship with me. He has the boys, you know, and I always had my nose in a book, anyway. I never worked on cars or played hockey or did anything interesting like that, so…" She laughs, and that dimple I haven't seen in too long pops on her cheek. "Though, if he knew I was friends with a player on his favorite NHL team, he might change his tune. Shane's husband plays for the Rangers. She's promised me the best seats in the house as soon as I can sneak away to a game."

"What do you have to sneak away from these

days?" I ask, both intrigued and saddened by this glimpse into her life. I want to know everything I've missed, and then I want to write her parents a cutting letter, telling them what absolute pieces of shit they've been.

"Just life," she says, vaguely. "Work and all the rest of it."

"What do you do? Have you taken the architectural world by storm yet?"

"What do you do?" she asks, dodging my question again. "You said you dropped out of school. Did you ever go back?"

"I did. I got a creative writing degree from a program in the U.K."

She smiles. "That's amazing. What do you write?"

"Oh, a little bit of everything. For money, it's mostly articles for magazines, but I have a few horror novels I can't sell, and I just landed my first major non-fiction book deal. I write as Nathan West because I refuse to put my father's last name on anything he might try to take credit for."

"Good for you," she says, looking genuinely happy for me. "That's incredible. I'm so proud of you, Nate."

"Thanks. But I would rather talk about you. You were always more interesting than I was, Einstein."

Her smile falters. "Oh, I was not. Don't be ridiculous."

"I'm not ridiculous." I crouch on the opposite side of the coffee table, bringing my face level with hers. "But I do get the feeling there's something you're not telling me."

She meets my gaze, but the shields are already slamming down, shutting me out again. "Yeah, well. Some things are better left untold."

"Because they hurt?" I ask gently.

"Because they're in the past and nothing can change them." She swallows before adding in a softer voice, "And yes. Because it would hurt."

"Maybe talking to someone would help?"

She laughs beneath her breath. "Therapy, you mean?"

I shrug and she lifts her gaze to the ceiling.

"Well, yes, Nate, I have considered therapy," she says. "And I'll probably consider it more seriously now that I know that your father is in possession of pictures of me without my shirt on."

I wince. "So that part had time to sink in, did it?"

"Oh yeah." She nods. "It sunk in, and my stomach isn't happy about it. But that could also be because I skipped breakfast."

"Want to order room service?" I jump at the chance to get us back on safer ground, realizing by now how easy it would be to scare Adeline away. "I hear they've got a killer grilled cheese with tomato salad. Eduardo had it for breakfast. Said it was the best hangover food he'd ever had."

"I don't have a hangover."

"I do," I confess. "I could barely sleep last night. I kept thinking of all the things I wanted to tell you and worrying I wouldn't get the chance." I sit down on the coffee table, facing her, close enough that our knees almost brush. "I'm glad we're talking again. I've missed you."

She studies my face, anxiety tightening her features. "What is this, Nate? What do you want?"

"I want to buy you lunch," I say, keeping my tone light. "And we don't have to talk anymore if you don't want to. We can turn on the TV and watch cheesy Valentine's Day movies. Or, I think the lodge has a visitor channel. We could listen to the history of the Valentine's Day tree and get a look at the hokey-pokey schedule."

"Don't play dumb," she whispers. "It doesn't suit you."

"Well, I'm not dumb, but I'm no Einstein," I joke, hoping it will make her smile.

"Neither am I. Not anymore." She stands, shaking her head with a sigh. "I should go, Nate. I don't know what I was thinking." She moves around the coffee table, but I swing my legs over and step into her path, cutting off her escape route.

"Don't go." I hold my hands up in surrender. "I'll back off, okay? I won't push. I just want to be around you, Addie. We can be friends if that's all you're up for, I just—"

"I can't be friends with you, Nate," she says, a humorless laugh bursting from her lips. "No. Just…no. It's not going to happen."

"Why not?"

Her jaw clenches. "I just can't. It won't work."

She tries to step around me again, but I shift in front of her. "I know I made mistakes, okay? I know that, but I'm—"

"It's not about your mistakes. It's not about you at all. It's about *me!*" She thumps a hand to her chest. "It can never be like it used to be. I can't talk to you anymore."

"We were talking just fine a minute ago!"

She shakes her head, sending her curls flying. "You don't get it. I can't *really* talk to you. I can't. I won't."

"Why not, Adeline? What—"

"Because I can't stand for you to know!"

"To know what?" I ask, frustration thickening the words.

"To know that I've done nothing," she shouts, tears rising in her eyes. "That I *am* nothing!"

"Jesus, Adeline. That's not true." I reach out, needing to wrap my arms around her. Her words are too painful for me to do anything else.

But she braces her fists on my chest, holding me at a distance "It *is* true, Nate. You don't know anything about me, or my life. Not anymore."

"Then tell me," I beg, trying to get her to look at me, to see that I'm on her side. "Please, Ad.

Talk to me. I'm not here to judge. If anyone deserves to be judged, it's me for being a fucking coward and leaving you alone, or your parents for being sanctimonious pieces of shit. You didn't do anything wrong. If your plans got messed up because your parents kicked you out of the house, that's their fault, not yours." I bend closer, dropping my voice. "Is that what happened?"

"I can't do this." She shakes her head again, but with less conviction. "I can't talk about it. I don't. To anyone."

"Then don't talk." I let my forehead rest lightly against hers, bringing my hands to cup her face. "Don't ever tell me if you don't want to. You decide what I deserve to know, but don't shut me out." I brush my thumb lightly back and forth across her cheek. "I know you feel it, too. The way it still is between us."

She sucks in a breath. "It's impossible."

"It's not." I thread my fingers into her hair, my pulse spiking as she shivers beneath my touch. "It's right. And it's good. And it can be even better." I kiss her forehead, letting my lips move against her skin as I whisper, "Just let me in, Adeline. Let me prove to you that you and Einstein were right. The most beautiful thing we can experience is the mysterious. And you've always been my favorite mystery."

She sobs softly, her head tipping back. "That's not playing fair."

"I'm not here to play fair," I whisper.

Her lips part, but I silence her with a kiss. After a moment that feels like forever, her arms go around my neck and her curves press against my chest and she kisses me back, sending relief rushing through my veins. Her tongue dances with mine, telling me all her secrets, and as I draw her back toward the couch, she silently promises that it's not too late.

That it's never too late for two people who are meant to be.

Chapter FIFTEEN

Adeline

For the first fifteen years of my life I was certain that I had it all together, and flawed characters who got swept off course by sex, drugs, alcohol, or their own inner demons had a hard time earning my sympathy. I believed that if you wanted to be the hero of your own story, then you would be. It was just a matter of saying no and meaning it, and then transferring your focus to healthier objects of fascination.

And then Nate kissed me, touched me, made me see stars during the daytime on a haunted beach where the ghosts of lovers drowned at sea were rumored to make the sand dunes glow after dark, and I learned how easy it was to be swept away. That's why I had my girlfriend pick up a few morning-after pills for me before she left for school. I knew how easy it would be to forget all my responsibilities and get lost in the incredible, magical, hot as hell things Nate made me feel.

Now, as he pulls me down onto the couch and lengthens his body on top of mine, I sense that I'm about to lose control all over again.

But before I do, I whisper against his lips, "Condom? In case I'm stupid enough to let this go that far?"

"Covered." His hands skim my curves over my clothes, making me burn as he cups my breast in his hand. "But it wouldn't be stupid. I won't let you down again, Einstein, and I promise to make you feel good."

My breath rushes out as he kisses his way down my throat. "You were always good at making me feel good."

"I can't wait to make you come for me, Adeline. You're so fucking beautiful when you come." He rolls my nipple through the fabric of my sweater dress, making me gasp as electricity rips through my nerve endings. It's like all the lamps in my quiet, dim little house are being thrown at once, making me squint in the fierce light exploding in the darkness. It's sudden and so violent that it almost hurts, but it doesn't because Nate kisses me, giving me a place to put all the need he sends thundering through me as he continues to play with my nipples through my dress.

"I dream about this all the time." He settles between my spread legs, letting me feel how hard he is beneath his jeans. "I dream about making love to you, and then wake up feeling like shit because I know I'll never touch you again."

"You're touching me now." I bite gently into his bottom lip as he grinds against me, rubbing between my legs, making my need spike hard and fast. I reach between us, finding the thick ridge of his erection, sighing as I stroke him through his jeans. "And now *I'm* touching you."

"Fuck, Addie." He groans, pressing into my hand. "You drive me crazy."

"Me, too." I nip his jaw this time, loving the way his breath catches as I slip the button at the top of his fly. "I want you. Right now."

"Not so fast." He captures my hands, pinning them to the couch above my head. "I need to make you come at least once first. And I really need the taste of you in my mouth."

"But I don't—" Before I can tell him that I don't want his mouth, I want his cock—that beautiful, hard, pulsing cock that leaves no doubt he wants me as desperately as I want him—he kisses me again.

This kiss is deeper and harder, showing me no mercy. He lays claim to every inch of my mouth as he reaches beneath my dress, pulling my panty hose and simple black briefs down around my knees. He doesn't pull away until I'm breathless, panting, clawing at his shoulders, his ass, his rock hard chest that feels even more powerful than it used to. In a matter of seconds, he has my left boot off and my leg free of panties and hose.

He doesn't bother with the other boot. As soon as he's able to spread my thighs, he guides them wide and settles between them.

I tense for a second, remembering there's some reason I don't want him to kiss me like this, but then his tongue is on my clit, warm and firm and wicked, and I forget everything but the way he makes me feel. I'm lightning in a bottle, a bonfire in the rain, the ocean surging onto shore only to evaporate the second it kisses the lava fields rolling down into the sea.

He makes me go hot and cold, dizzy and clear, sane and out of my mind all at once.

"You taste the same," he murmurs between my legs, his tongue dipping into where I am shamefully wet for him. "God, Addie, I want to tattoo the taste of you on my tongue."

"Oh, God. God, yes," I chant as the pressure builds between my hips.

"Are you going to come on my mouth, Einstein?" There's a smug note in his voice that should probably bother me, but hell, the man knows what he's doing. Who am I to fault him for realizing he's the master of oral sex?

"Yes!" I fist my fingers in his hair. "I'm so close, so fucking close."

"I love hearing you cuss." His tongue sweeps up the center of me, making me gasp. "Tell me how fucking close you are again, Addie. Talk dirty to me in that sweet voice of yours."

"I'm so close. Fuck me with your mouth, Nate. Fuck me harder."

Nate growls something that sounds filthy and approving and devotes himself to devouring me with a single-minded passion I can feel dancing across every nerve in my body. I spread my legs wider, pulsing into him as he consumes me, licking and sucking and biting until I'm wild. And then he drives his fingers inside, hitting that place he magically knows how to find, and I detonate.

I cry his name and tighten my grip in his hair, holding him to me as I come, rocking my hips into his mouth as he hums and cusses and insists that I'm the sexiest woman in the world.

And in that moment…I am.

Me—fades into the wallpaper, boringly accommodating, dour librarian casual Adeline Klein—*I* am the sexiest woman in the world. I'm flying so high I don't hesitate to reach for the close of Nate's pants and rip down his zipper. "Take off your pants," I demand as he kisses me again, the salt-and-woman essence of my body on his tongue.

Nate's right; it does taste good, especially with his flavor mingling with it.

"Pants off," I insist, shoving at the waistband. "Now."

"I want you to be sure." He slips his fingers back between my legs, making me moan as I rock into his touch. "It doesn't have to go further than this, Addie. We don't have to rush. I can make you come and you can remember that I'm good for something other than being a pain in your ass."

"You were never a pain in my ass," I say, lips parting as the pleasure begins to build again. "I loved you. I loved being in love with you and spending time with you and fucking you."

He groans. "Seriously, Addie, hearing you cuss is almost more than I can take. Why is it so hot?"

"Because when we were together before, I was a girl who was too shy to say things like that." My breath catches as I screw my courage to the begging him to screw me point. "I'm still shy, sometimes, but I'm not a girl. So you'd better take your pants off and fuck me, Nate, before I go find someone who won't be so worried about rushing me."

He pulls back, a dark, dangerous look in his eyes that makes me shiver. "Yes, ma'am, Ms. Klein. But you're going to wait two seconds while I get a condom."

I nod, the mention of the condom clearing some of the fog from my thoughts.

He pulls away, tugging off his sweater and starting on the buttons of his shirt as he backs away. "By the time I get back from the bathroom, I want you naked, beautiful. I'm flipping the deadbolt so we won't be disturbed. Ed isn't due back for another hour, at least, but I may not be finished fucking you by then." He strips off his shirt and tosses it on the floor, revealing his incredible, beautiful, perfect chest. "We've got a lot of making up for lost time to do."

With a wink he turns and disappears into the bathroom. The second he vanishes, I leap to my feet, struggling back into my underwear and pantyhose, heart pounding fast and panicked against my ribs.

What the hell was I thinking? I can't get naked with Nate!

I have to get out of here. Now! Ten minutes ago would be better. I need to rewind time and prevent myself from getting completely out of control. I should never have let him kiss me. I should have done whatever it took to keep my lips from his. I should have eaten a raw onion and put a bag over my head if that's what it took.

A door slams in the bathroom, and I jump, glancing guiltily around for my purse only to remember I didn't bring it with me. I pat the front pocket of my dress, realize my room key is still safely where I left it, and make a run for the door.

I literally run, dashing past the bathroom, knowing speed is my only chance. Stealth won't work. Nate is probably sliding that condom on right now and if I get a look at him in all his naked glory there's a good chance I'll go out of my head again and do something even stupider than I have already.

I reach the door and haul it open, just as Nate calls out, "Adeline?" But I don't answer; I lunge through the door, ramming into a solid wall of papa bear. I bounce off Eduardo's chest with an *oof*, landing on my ass back in the hotel room.

"Adeline!" He claps his hands, grinning like I've just completed some impressive trick and not fallen flat on my rear. "Oh, I'm so glad to see you here. You'll be thrilled to learn that Nathaniel is now a free man!"

"What? What about Max and pool boy?" Nate appears beside me, still shirtless, but thankfully with his jeans firmly buttoned and zipped.

Eduardo's eyebrows lift as he takes in the gun and six pack show. "Oh dear. Should I come back later, loves? Tomorrow morning, perhaps?"

"No," I say at the exact moment Nate says, "Yes."

Eduardo's brows arch higher. "Well, I'm not sure how to take that, but as far as Max and his pool boy are concerned, Max cornered me in the spa about half an hour ago." His eyes dance as his shoulders shimmy. "I won't go into graphic detail, but suffice it to say there was begging and it was done on his knees. His knees!"

"All right!" Nate holds out a hand, which Eduardo high fives.

"He insisted he's realized the error of his ways and is desperate to have me back." The older man laughs wickedly. "I told him to go home and sign the paperwork giving me full ownership of the salons, and that we would talk reconciliation next week, after my lawyer has had a chance to look things over."

"But you're not taking him back," Nate says.

"Oh God no, sweet pea. I'm going to take my money and run singing nah nah nah nah boo boo, all the way down Fifth Avenue." Eduardo crosses his arms and leans against the doorframe with a happy sigh. "So, my darlings, I'm a happy man and it's all because of this gorgeous creature who made Max so exquisitely jealous. As my way of saying thank you, I would love to set you two up in the honeymoon suite for the rest of the weekend. I think you deserve a beautiful place for your reunion."

"That's very sweet of you," I say, coming to my feet and smoothing my dress down. "But Nate and I have decided to take things slow. Isn't that right, Nate?"

He falters, but after a second he nods. "Of course. If that's what you want."

"It is," I say, smiling as I slip around Eduardo and out into the hall. "That just seems best, you know? Taking things slow and easy and um…" I jab a thumb down the hall. "So I'm going to go. But maybe we can have breakfast tomorrow?"

"Absolutely. I'll be waiting in the lobby at seven. Come down whenever you're ready." Nate looks so relieved that I feel terrible about lying, but I can't help it. I just have to get him to let me go without his deploying another diabolical kiss attack. "But you're welcome to have dinner with us, tonight, too. Or at least hang out for celebratory drinks. I think this calls for mojitos in the hot tub, right, Ed?"

"Yes!" Ed claps again. "Oh, do join us for mojitos. A celebration is always more festive with three."

"I appreciate the offer, but I really am tired. It's been a long time since I've been…out in the elements." I see Nate smile out of the corner of my eye, but don't look his way. The less I look at that man, the better. "But congratulations on your good news, Eduardo. I'm so happy that everything worked out."

"Me, too, doll." He casts an assessing look my direction. "I think everyone deserves a happy ending, don't you?"

"Of course," I agree, wiggling my fingers as I back away. "See you tomorrow."

"See you tomorrow, Einstein," Nate says in a soft, sexy voice, so sweet and confusing that I can't think about it too much.

With a final thumbs-up, I turn and walk down the hall, deliberately not thinking about happy endings or old flames or anything else that might keep me from making a calm, clean, reasonably paced getaway.

Chapter SIXTEEN

Adeline

I manage to keep my jittery legs and panic under control until I round the corner from Nate and Eduardo's room and hit a stretch of long, abandoned hallway. But as soon as I'm out of their line of sight, I break into a jog, rushing quietly toward the opposite side of the lodge, calculating how long it will take me to pack and what the chances are of convincing a cab to come pick me up in this weather.

I have to get out of here. *Now.*

I have to get away from Nate before my luck runs out and he succeeds in getting me out of my clothes.

The truth is written all over my skin. The second he sees the scar, he'll know. I could lie and say I had my appendix removed or donated a kidney or had part of my liver stolen after a date with a man I met on Yes, Cupid went seriously, organ-harvestingly wrong, but Nate will see through me.

He's right. It's just like it used to be. The connection between us is intense and real, and there's no way I'll be able to look into his eyes and make him believe a lie.

But I can't tell him the truth, either. At least not now. I don't think I could get the words out, even if I tried. After seven years of stuffing that dark, ugly story down to the bottom of my mind, it's well and truly stuck. And now that Nate has brought the past crashing into my present, I realize that the monster inside me hasn't been idle. It hasn't been hiding out in a corner taking naps; it's been gorging itself, growing even bigger and uglier than it was before.

Turns out shadow things don't need light or air to survive. They thrive in the dark, feeding on silence, shame, and isolation. And I've been all those things. Alone. Ashamed. And silent—because I thought silence was a way to show that I was strong.

But it wasn't, and I'm not strong. I'm weak, so weak all it would take is a gust of wind to make me shatter.

Nate is right, I should have found someone to talk to. Maybe it would have helped and I wouldn't feel so out of control right now. I don't know. All I know is that I'm afraid that if I open that locked door, my secret will rush out like an ogre with hammers for fists, smashing everything in its path.

I can't let that happen while Nate is around. If I do, I'll ruin any hope for a future with him in it. I want to believe he's right, that there's a way back to the dream I was so certain was lost forever, but I'm not ready yet. I need time to put the past to rest before I reach for the future.

As I pass through the lobby, I glance out the windows at the storm, nibbling at my bottom lip. The snow is coming down so hard that I can't see past the first few feet of the lake. The ice-skating rink at the top of the hill and the mountains in the distance are whited-out, erased by the swirling flakes. If I'm going to get off the mountain before this storm becomes a full-fledged blizzard, I'm going to have to hurry.

Figuring the sooner I call a cab the better, I swing by the concierge desk, smiling at the woman in the Tomahawk Mountain House fleece, whose nametag reads "Francine" in gold letters.

"Hello, Francine," I say, still breathless from my dash down the hall and six flights of stairs. "I was wondering if you could call me a cab to New Paltz. I'll be ready to go in about twenty minutes. I just have to pop upstairs and grab my things."

Her thin, white eyebrows draw closer together. "Oh, sweetheart, I don't know if they'll be able to get up here in this weather, even with four-wheel drive. And you'll have an even harder time getting back from town this evening. The storm isn't supposed to let up until tomorrow."

"I'm not coming back. I'm going to stay in New Paltz tonight and look for a rental car tomorrow. I have to get back to the city sooner than expected."

"I hope it's nothing serious." She taps her fingers on the top of her phone, but doesn't pick up the receiver.

"It's not serious, but it's urgent," I say firmly. It's nice that she's a kind person who cares about strangers taking risks on treacherous mountain roads, but I'm willing to risk a little snow and ice in exchange for the peace of mind of knowing I'm far away from Nate, with my secrets still locked up tight. "I really do have to get back. I'm willing to pay the driver extra for the trouble."

"All right, I'll see what I can do, honey. Give me a minute," she says, punching a red button for an outside line. "But just so you know, the highway into the city might not be passable tomorrow. Our crews around here do a great job with the roads in town and up to the hotels, but the state doesn't get in a hurry. They might not get to clearing the highway until the day after tomorrow. Maybe even later."

"I understand. Thank you for checking for me, anyway. I appreciate it."

While she dials, I step to the end of the desk, contemplating the increasingly aggressive snow outside. I suppose I could go back to the "hiding out in my room" plan, but my gut says that Nate will find a way to track me down. He might decide to bang on every door in the hotel, knowing him. He can be stubborn when he's got his mind set on something, and he clearly has his mind set on me.

Poor you!

You know most women would give an arm, a leg, and an eyeball or two to have Nate chasing them around a romantic lodge on Valentine's Day, right?

"Most women don't have the history I have with him," I mumble.

"What's that, dear?" Francine asks from behind me.

I turn with a smile. "Nothing, just talking to myself. Sorry."

She grins. "No need to apologize. I talk to myself all the time. I'm very good company." She winks as she holds out a piece of paper. "All right, I've got a guy willing to pick you up. Very safe driver, four-wheel drive pickup, with chains on the tires. No extra charge."

I sigh with relief, but Francine doesn't give me time to thank her before she warns, "But he'll only go as far as the top of the hill. He's been stuck at the bottom of our drive before and won't risk it. One of the valets will drive you up to meet him by the lodge entrance. They've got the four-wheel drive UTV out there all gassed up and ready to go."

"Perfect!" I check the clock on the wall. "So I

should be out there in twenty minutes?"

"Better make it thirty," she says. "Hank said it will probably take him double the usual time to get up the mountain. So be sure to bundle up in case it takes him longer and you end up waiting."

"Thanks so much, Francine." I cling tight to the slip of paper with the driver's name and number on it. "I appreciate it so much. You're a lifesaver."

"Oh, no, don't say that, honey," she says, a troubled look creasing her features. "I feel bad enough sending you out in this weather without risking a jinx on top of it. You just take care of yourself and drive safe tomorrow if you decide to risk the highway, okay?"

"Will do." With a final wave, I turn and dash up the main staircase.

Twenty minutes later, I've changed back into my ski clothes—with my coat buttoned up tight this time—packed my meager belongings into the laundry bag housekeeping left in the closet, and hurried back down to the lobby. Outside at the valet station, I have to shout to be heard over the wind wailing through the eaves of the roof. The man in charge of the UTV raises an eyebrow when I tell him I need a lift up to the entrance, but when I assure him a cab is coming to meet me, he wraps his scarf around his head a few more times and tells me to hop in.

The ride up the drive is miserable, but I'm so relieved to be moving farther away from Nate that I don't mind the flakes stinging into my eyes or the wind threatening to rip my new hat off and deliver it to the mountain gods as a sacrifice. I simply hold on to my cap, clench my jaw against the cold, and try not to shiver too obnoxiously, hoping we won't have to wait long for my driver to arrive.

But luck is on my side for once. When we reach the top of the hill, a black pickup truck with a "Hank's Cab Service" sign in the window is already idling near the lodge entrance, emitting comforting puffs of smoke from its tailpipe.

I thank the valet, tip him my last five-dollar bill, and climb into the passenger's seat of the truck to find an old man with faded blue eyes waiting for me with a smile on his face. "There you are. Adeline, I assume?"

"Yes, sir." I brush the snow from my coat as I buckle up.

"Hank." He holds out his hand, giving mine a firm shake.

"Thanks so much for coming to pick me up, Hank. I really appreciate it."

"You can thank Francine when we get to town. She's the only one who can get me out of the house once I've settled in for the night." He shifts the truck into drive and checks his rearview mirror before pulling out onto the road. "She made me promise to give her a call when we get to New Paltz. She wants to know you made it down the mountain safe and sound."

"She's sweet," I say, settling my purse on my lap.

"She is," he agrees with a nod. "That's why I married her. Though, the fact that she's the prettiest thing I've ever seen doesn't hurt, either. We're celebrating forty years next month."

"Congratulations." I smile, liking that Francine is still the prettiest woman in the world to the man who loves her. "So I'm guessing she wants you to get to town safe, too."

"She's still tolerating me after all this time, so I suppose so." He slows as we round the first corner and head into the wind. Snow churns wildly against the glass, making it hard to see more than a few feet in front of the truck.

I tense, but before I can ask if we should turn around, Hank adds, "We'll be fine. Just gotta take it slow." He reaches out, cranking up the heat. "I've been driving these mountains my whole life and never spun out. The secret is not to get in a rush. You don't have an appointment in town, do you?"

I shake my head. "No. Just hoping to find an empty room somewhere not too expensive. I'm going to be renting a car tomorrow to drive back to the city."

He grunts. "So maybe something near the rental car place. They use to have an Enterprise in the parking lot of the La Quinta, but I don't—"

His words are cut off by an ugly *thudda crunch* as the truck suddenly jerks hard to the right and the driver's side window implodes.

I scream, grabbing onto the handle over my window as freezing air rushes in and the truck careens across the road, spinning in wild circles as whatever hit us skids away into the near-darkness.

"Hank!" I cry out as he collapses over the steering wheel. "Hank! Wake up! Hank!"

I reach for my seat belt, planning to dive across and try to get control of the wheel, but the button won't release. I try again and again, fighting with the nylon holding me prisoner as the truck continues to spin and the wind continues to howl and my heart pounds so hard it's like a fist slamming into my ribs from the inside.

And then suddenly there's a strange gulp of silence, like fate taking a breath, bracing itself to finish this off. To finish me, and poor Hank, all because I didn't know how to let go of the past before it was too late.

"I'm sorry," I sob, but my voice is barely audible over the scream of metal as the truck bursts through the guardrail and starts to fall.

Chapter SEVENTEEN

From the texts of Nathaniel Casey
and Mitch McKibbon

Mitch: Hey, it's Mitch. This is my new number.
Do you have a minute?

Nate: A minute or two, but I might not be with
you for long.
I'm in the middle of a snowstorm and service is
getting patchy.

Mitch: A snowstorm in the city?

Nate: No, I'm out near New Palz, at that
Victorian hotel in the mountains that Stephanie
says is haunted.

Mitch: Ah, Tomahawk. It's totally haunted, man.

Nate: Meh. I read about it. The white lady in the attic sounds contrived, and the hotel has no creep vibe. It's as wholesome as Christmas morning with extra sugar cookies.

Mitch: I'm not talking about the white lady. I'm talking about this couple that went full on Shining back when the hotel was still under construction. The authorities found their bodies in a cabin near the edge of the property.
For years people thought they'd pulled a Romeo and Juliet because she was an heiress and her parents were trying to break up the marriage, but forensic tests on the bones years later proved that it was a double murder.
Dude stabbed her, and then she shot him with a shotgun. They might have survived, at least the girl, since the knife didn't hit anything vital, but there had been an avalanche earlier that night. She made it to the door, but she couldn't dig herself out of the cabin in time to get help. Poor kid bled out on the porch.
Locals say sometimes the snow near the old cabin still turns red just before sunset and you can hear people screaming inside the crumbling walls.
Whooooo-hoooooo…
ghost emoji
stabbing knife emoji
skull emoji

Nate: Riveting, but I'm assuming that's not what

you texted about.

Mitch: What's wrong with you, man? You usually can't get enough of this kind of stuff. Am I on your shit list for some reason?

Nate: No. Sorry. I'm just…distracted.
I finished up a job today for that consulting firm I've been working for part time, and I need to go take care of some personal stuff.

Mitch: Personal stuff like a girl?

Nate: Yes. A girl.
The girl, actually…

Mitch: Shut up! THE girl? The one your dad hated so much he threatened to have you thrown in jail for kiddie porn?

Nate: Yeah. We randomly ran into other again, but it doesn't feel random. It's like fucking fate, or something…

Mitch: I'm not sure I believe in fate, but that's cool.

Nate: No, it's not cool. It's messed up. She's clearly had a shit time of things since we split, and all signs point to it being at least partly my fault. And now I hate myself for letting so much time go by without making sure she was okay.

Because she's special.

Really special.

And I don't believe in fate, either, by the way. Or I didn't before this weekend. But there are too many coincidences for this to just be something that's happening. It's something that's *meant* to happen, Mitchell.

I'm one hundred percent for real about this, not fucking joking, so don't say something dismissive that's going to piss me off.

Mitch: Have you been drinking?

Nate: No….

But maybe I should start…

I'm wound up, man. I can't shake this feeling that something's about to go wrong. Or maybe it's already gone wrong. That maybe I've screwed things up with her, and she's never going to give me another chance.

What if today was my one shot and I fucked it all up?

Mitch: Okay, don't start drinking. Drinking would be bad for you right now.

You should take a hot shower, meditate, and find some stars to look at.

You know stars always bring you back from the edge.

Nate: The sun hasn't set on this side of the world, and it's snowing too hard for stars.
Besides, that won't work anymore because I remembered the Carl Sagan quote.

Mitch: The Carl Sagan quote...

Nate: "For small creatures such as we, the vastness is bearable only through love."
It's not bearable anymore, Mitch.
Not without her, and maybe it never was.
Maybe I've been kidding myself all these years, thinking I had my shit together. I don't know anymore. All I know is that it feels like I've been sleepwalking through life, and then yesterday I saw her and I woke up and now there's no going back.

Mitch: Yesterday...
So you've been back at this thing with summer-love girl for two days?

Nate: I don't want to hear it.
Fate, Mitchell! Fate doesn't care about your dating rules, or how much time I've been back in contact with Addie, so don't even start.

Mitch: All right, all right! Message received.
And hey, what do I know anyway? It's not like I've ever made a relationship work.
That's actually what I wanted to talk to you

about. I'm heading back to the city tomorrow night. I've decided to tell my parents I'm gay.

Nate: You're gay?

Mitch: Seriously, dude?

Nate: But I thought you said all the women you've tried to date weren't into the Eat, Pray, Love thing?

Mitch: I said all the PEOPLE I've been trying to date. I never said women.

Nate: Are you sure?

Mitch: Yes, I'm sure! And you totally know that I'm gay! Remember the time in Greece when Abe and I were making out at the discotheque right in front of you?

Nate: I thought that was the ouzo. We all drank a LOT of ouzo that night.

Mitch: Ouzo doesn't make people gay, Nate. It makes your mouth taste like someone took a black-licorice-scented dump on your tongue.

Nate: God, don't remind me.
Sorry I didn't get it. But in my defense, after Monty made out with that donkey outside the

club, that became my dominant memory of the evening. And a major reason why I avoid discotheques like the plague.

Mitch: And there's the fact that you can't dance worth a shit.

Nate: Agreed.
So…you're gay.

Mitch: Yes, I'm fucking gay. Thanks for not noticing.
Way to make me even more stressed about coming out to my parents. All this time, I thought you were one of the few people who was in the know and was cool with it.

Nate: Hey! I am cool! Don't be stressed. It's all good, man.
It doesn't make a difference to me whether you like dick or pussy, you're still my favorite asshole, and that's all that matters.

Mitch: Thanks, man.
I appreciate that. Seriously.

Nate: Of course. And I'm back in the city on Tuesday night. I'll be around for beers and moral support if coming out to the family doesn't go the way you hope it will.

Mitch: Well, I'm hoping my father will have a heart attack and my mother will finally be free of that drunk, wife-beating son of bitch and have a chance to think for herself. So if you've got any heart-attack vibes to spare, send them my pop's way.

Nate: Done. I won't go to hell for that, right?

Mitch: You're already there, man.
If hell isn't a ridiculous world like this, I don't know what is.

Nate: It doesn't have to be ridiculous, Mitch.
Sometimes it makes sense.
    Like when I'm with her.

Mitch: Then, I'm happy for you.
I hope you and summer love girl live happily ever after.

Nate: Her name is Adeline. Hopefully you'll get the chance to meet her. She lives in the city, too.

Mitch: Adeline? You're shitting me…
That girl I was texting is named Adeline, and she was at a lodge with her ex named Nate! What are that chances, right? I mean, your name isn't anything special, but Adeline is weird and old-fashioned and how many exes are trapped together at a hotel on Valentine's Day?

But she was under the impression her ex was gay, so maybe it's not the same girl.

Five minutes later...

Mitch: But I saved her number when I tossed the phone I...*ahem*...borrowed.
I was planning to text her and apologize. I'll ask her if her Nate matches your stupid-pretty description just in case. What's your real last name again? I always forget.
I know West is the pen name, but...

Ten minutes later...

Mitch: Well, I guess I lost you.
Stay safe in the storm, man. And thanks for the beer offer. I appreciate it.
Good luck with Adeline, too. I hope it works out. I really do.

From the texts of Pervert in Paris
and Adeline Klein

Unknown Number: Hey Adeline, this is the Pervert in Paris.
BEFORE YOU BLOCK ME, I know it's creepy that I'm texting, but the only reason I wrote down your number was so I could apologize for being a dick to you before. I was writing an article on Why Women Love Assholes and took my

research too far, and I'm sorry. I promise never to use a phone that isn't mine to text jerky things to anyone ever again.

I'm actually a nice person. Mostly.

Anyway, I hope you'll forgive me. Especially considering we might have a friend in common. My friend Nate West—can't remember his real last name, but that's his pen name—was just talking about a woman named Adeline. If he's the ex you were texting about before, then there must be some sort of misunderstanding. Nate is as straight as they come, a really great guy, and it sounds like he's completely gone on you. I normally wouldn't violate the bro code by sharing that kind of information, but I figure I owe you a solid, and it might make you feel better if it's the same Nate. Maybe hit me back and let me know? Hope all is good with you.

Wishing you happy things,

Pervert, aka Mitch

Chapter EIGHTEEN

Nate

I pace to the window, holding my phone up closer to the ceiling, but there's not a bar in sight and my last text message to Mitch refuses to send.

That's her! That's my Adeline! There was a misunderstanding and she thought I was romantically involved with the friend I'm here with. But that's totally her! Don't you see what this means?

THIS IS FATE!

WHAT ARE THE FUCKING CHANCES THAT THE PHONE YOU HAPPENED TO STEAL IN PARIS JUST HAPPENS TO BELONG TO MY EX-GIRLFRIEND'S BEST FRIEND!? THERE ARE BILLIONS AND BILLIONS OF PEOPLE IN THE WORLD, MITCHELL. SHIT LIKE THIS DOESN'T JUST HAPPEN!!

But it's happening to Adeline and me, and I believe that means something.

It fucking means something, and I'm not letting her go without a fight this time.

"Everything okay?" Eduardo asks from behind me, where he's perched on the couch watching the Weather Channel predict dire things for the Catskills in the next twenty-four hours.

"Yeah," I say, then I shake my head. "No. I feel sick to my stomach."

"Completely understandable. This is all very strange, Nathaniel, I won't argue with you there. But it's also wonderful, and unless I'm very mistaken, I think it means that everything is going to work out the way it should have years ago, before you and your girl lost each other."

I turn from the window, crossing my arms at my chest. "I want to believe that, but I've got this feeling that something's wrong. That she's not okay, or she's in trouble, or..." I sigh. "I don't know. I'm probably being crazy."

"You're not being crazy." Eduardo stands, joining me near the doors, gazing out at the frenzy of snow pelting the world outside. "You're probably just picking up on Addie's 'get me the hell out of here' vibes."

"What?" I turn to him with a frown.

"Oh, honey, I'm surprised Adeline didn't break into a sprint on her way down the hall. That little girl was in full-on flight-or-fight mode. She was running from you as fast as her legs could carry her."

I curse, running a clawed hand through my hair. "So I fucked it up? Is that what you're saying?"

"No, not at all," Eduardo says. "She cares about you. One look at her and you can see that there are still feelings there, but she's also scared, sweet pea. She's clearly been through some ugly stuff. So she might need to run from you for a little while, and that's okay. Your job is to figure out when to give her space and when to get close enough to let her know that you're not going to give up on her."

"I shouldn't have kissed her." I curse again. "I should have taken it slow."

Addie might have been talking dirty to me, but she was also crying and upset, and I've never seen Adeline cry like that. She's not the kind of person who gets upset easily, or at least she didn't used to be. The fact is I don't know what she's been through or who she is now. The connection between us is still there, but the communication isn't. And until it is, I should have trusted the voice in my head that said the best way forward was to keep things light and give her space.

"I don't know about that," Eduardo says, breaking into my thoughts. "A kiss is always a good thing, but maybe stripping down was a little much. That chest of yours isn't for the faint of heart, pumpkin." He winks, and I almost laugh, but I don't because nothing's funny right now.

"I should go apologize." I glance back at the door, ready to run after her right now. "But fuck, I didn't get her room number. Or the name she's registered under. Or her cell phone. Why didn't I get her fucking—" I break off, inspiration striking. "But Mitch has it. He said he wrote it down! I just have to find a place where this stupid phone can get some reception and call him back."

"Excellent plan," Eduardo says. "But if you can't get service, you'll be able to see Adeline in the morning. And she might feel better after a good night's sleep. In any event, I think I should add her name to our reservation for dinner tomorrow night. That way, if she's still feeling skittish, I can play chaperone and put her at ease. And if you two are ready for a romantic Valentine's Day dinner, I can make myself scarce and you lovebirds can enjoy yourselves."

"Good idea, and thank you so much," I say, starting toward the door. "I'll take care of changing the reservation. I'm going out hunting for bars, anyway. I can swing by the concierge while I'm out."

"All right." Eduardo sighs, stretching his arms overhead. "And I will take this opportunity to grab a quick victory nap before we go rustle up mojitos. Revenge is lovely, but exhausting. Happy hunting, doll."

"Happy napping." I slip out into the hall, making a mental note to tell Bash that I want my portion of this intervention to be on the house.

Eduardo is starting to feel more like a friend than a client, and after he's been so willing to play cupid between Addie and me, the least I can do is comp my fee.

For the first time in my writer life, I'm actually doing fine money-wise. Between the interventions and the book advance, I've got a cozy nest egg built up. Maybe, if all goes well, I can use some of it to take Addie on a trip, just the two of us, somewhere we can relax on the beach, take our time getting to know each other again, and do lots of lounging semi-naked together in the sun.

It's a nice daydream, but that's all it is—a dream.

As I move down the hallway toward the lobby, the "something's wrong" feeling returns, and a soft voice at the back of my mind assures me that unless I pull my head out of my ass, I won't be taking Addie anywhere.

"I'm trying to pull my head out of my ass," I mumble. "Just tell me what I'm supposed to do."

But the universe or fate or whatever force is behind the coincidences that keep binding Addie and me closer together isn't talking. There are no signs or omens, just an empty elevator with a note taped to the wall announcing that hokey-pokey has been cancelled due to lack of interest.

Chapter NINETEEN

Adeline

My head hurts and I'm cold. So cold.

Cold like the bottom of an arctic river where the fish are buried in the mud, waiting out the long, hard winter.

I open my eyes, stroking my hands through the icy water. My joints feel sleepy and my fingers are starting to go numb, but I don't stop; I pull harder, forcing my sluggish limbs to move. I'm not in trouble yet, but I have to find a hole in the ice before I run out of air, have to keep swimming because stillness equals death.

But all around me the world is quiet and blue, and I'm starting to feel so tired.

Tired and peaceful.

There's no reason to be scared, the current murmurs, *Look at the seaweed waving like an old friend. Listen to the rush of the waves and remember how good it feels to take it easy. Soft and quiet and easy…*

Yes. Easy can be good. There's a time for easy. A time for letting go of the past and the pain and letting your heart go blissfully numb.

But you heart just woke up again, Addie. It's not time to sleep. This time the voice in my head is my own, but younger, newer—the voice of a girl who has big dreams and so much to live for. *Wake up, Addie! Please! You're worth fighting for, and so is he.*

Nate's face flickers through my mind, and I try to swim again, but my arms refuse to play nice. They jerk through the water, twitching and trembling, until I'm shivering so hard my jaw threatens to chatter open and let the river rush down my throat.

If only I could find a place to rest for a little while, to curl up in the dark and just…

Close my eyes…

For a minute or two…

Addie! You can't go to sleep. If you do, you won't wake up!

Young me is right. I kick harder, clawing at the water as my nose stings and my eyes begin to burn from the cold. But the smooth gray surface of the ice is still so far away, and I'm so heavy. There are lead weights around my ankles, a cartoon anvil on my chest, rocks sewn into my clothes…

Rocks, rocks sewn into my clothes, I sing softly. *And where the rocks go nobody knows. And when the girl sinks who will care, only the fish and the waves and the…*

Hmmm… What rhymes with care?

My thoughts are so fuzzy…

Maybe…air? Yes. *Only the fish and the waves and the air.*

Satisfied that I've accomplished something, even if it's not what I originally intended, I curl my legs into my chest and draw the soaked winter coat I decided to wear swimming around me like a soggy cocoon.

But you're already a butterfly, Einstein. A deeper, softer voice drifts through the water, making it feel a bit warmer. *No cocoons for you. Wake up, beautiful. Come back to me. We don't end like this. Not this time.*

Nate. I think his name and my chest fills with pressure. *But I'm so tired. Tired and full of monsters.*

He hums, and the waves vibrate around me. *Well, good thing I'm not scared of monsters. You know that. And you aren't, either. You're one of the bravest people I've ever met.*

Not I'm not. But I uncurl, reaching my hands up toward the light, wondering if maybe it's not quite as far as I thought to the surface. *And I'm not a butterfly; I'm a caterpillar who crawled into a chrysalis and never came out.*

Maybe it's just taking you a little longer than the other caterpillars. There's nothing wrong with that.

I flutter my legs, experimenting with movement as my lips curve. *Are you saying I'm a special needs caterpillar?*

I'm dyslexic, he says, dodging the question. *It*

makes proofreading a son of a bitch. I can never catch all the errors, no matter how hard I try. But I keep trying, because I don't want my mistakes to get in the way of the story.

I swoop my arms through the water in a long, slow arc. *I made mistakes that got in the way. And I made another mistake when I jumped into this river. Why did I decide to go swimming in winter with my clothes on?* I pull and kick, frogging my way slowly toward the surface. *And how am I holding my breath for this long? Do you think I grew gills while I was in my chrysalis?*

That would be a good superhero origin story, Gill Girl, he says. *But I doubt it. I think it's more likely that you're not underwater.*

My arms go still. I stare at my spread fingers, wiggling them through the waves, but he's right—there's no resistance, no slippery feel of water. Only cold.

Wake up, Addie. His voice is louder, and the teasing note has vanished. *Wake up and help me get our story back on track. I love you.*

***

"Love, too," I mumble as my eyes creak open and pain flashes through my head.

I groan, pressing my hands into the hard plastic beneath my cheek, my thoughts racing. Where the hell am I, and why is it so flipping cold?

I blink, pulling into focus the handle of a car door and chunky pieces of ice scattered over the seat.

No, not ice—what's left of the window, I realize as I unbuckle my seat belt. There are pieces of it all over my hands and in my hair, and there's a gaping hole where the passenger's side window used to be, letting in wind and snow. It's freezing in here and getting colder. I can barely feel my nose, my fingers are numb, and my head is foggy in a way that scares me.

I bring my hand to my forehead, wincing as I discover a lump near my hairline. It hurts, but it's not that big or that bad. I should be able to think, to decide what to do next, but it's like my synapses are firing in slow motion.

For a long time the winter scene outside the shattered glass—the hill sloping down, the trees covered in white, the snow falling so fast, but eerily silent—makes no sense to me. It takes forever to remember that I've been in an accident and a second eternity to recall that I wasn't alone when the vehicle was hit.

I glance over my shoulder, pulling in a sharp breath as I see the older man slumped over the steering wheel.

I reach out, touching his shoulder. "Ha… Ha… Hank!" His name stutters to the front of my mind as I give him a gentle shake. "Hank! Hank are you… Are you…"

I can't finish the question. There's no point. If he's dead, he's not going to tell me. If he's dead, he's dead, and it will be my fault for deciding to run away in the middle of a blizzard.

Oh God, please. Please, be okay, I silently beg as I pull off my glove and touch his cool neck with bare fingers. It takes a long, gut-wrenching moment, but finally I feel a faint pulse beneath the skin.

Breath rushing out, I promise, "It's okay, I'll call for help."

I turn back to my side of the cab, searching for my purse, but all I find are a lipstick, at least twenty dollars in loose change, soggy receipts on the floor, a spilled coffee cup leaking pale brown liquid between the seats, and a random assortment of pens, screws, and one tiny flashlight wedged between the dash and the front window.

The truck is only tilting slightly to the right, but the chaos all around me makes me wonder...

I look up, see the deep dent in the roof, and swallow hard. We've been upside down. At least once. Do I remember that? I think maybe I do. I think I might have screamed and reached my arms up to brace myself, but it's all blurry. Blur and fog, shadow and shade, cold and numb, and if I don't get moving, I'm going to die here.

The realization cuts through the haze, making my pulse beat faster.

Coming onto my knees, I turn to look into the small passenger area behind the front seat. I find more detritus from my purse—a subway card and a bottle of hand sanitizer—but no sign of my cell phone. Thankfully, however, there is also a blanket and a large flashlight. It's getting dark and I'm going to need that flashlight to find my way back to the lodge and call for help.

"I'll be back as soon as I can," I say, wrapping the blanket around Hank's shoulders for extra warmth. "Or someone will be. I'm going to get help." For a moment, I debate lying Hank down on the seat so he'll be more comfortable, but decide it's best not to move him since I don't know exactly how badly he's injured. So I tuck the blanket around his shoulders and gently under his forehead instead, and with a silent promise not to let him down, I reach for the door handle.

It takes some shoving, but eventually the door opens and I spill out into the snow, hissing as my legs sink into the drift up to my thighs. Thank God I put my ski pants back on. Now, they might prove vital to staying alive long enough to get help.

Trudging through the snow to the front of the truck, I look up the mountain, my stomach lurching as I see the deep gash in the snow and the flattened baby trees where the truck rolled down the side of the hill. It looks too ugly for there to be two survivors down here, but so far we're both still breathing, and I mean to keep it that way.

But damn, it's a long way up to the road. At least five hundred feet, all of it uphill, and the last ten feet are a vertical climb up snow-covered rocks. Just looking at it makes my shivering arms feel like jelly, makes me wish I loved exercise as much as I love books, or that I'd kept rock climbing after I moved to the city. If so, maybe I would feel up to conquering the mountain, instead of seriously doubting whether I'll make it halfway up before what energy I've got left runs out.

"No time for doubt, Addie," I mutter, flicking on the flashlight. "Keep moving, one foot in front of the other." I'm starting up the hill when something in my peripheral vision catches my eye. I turn to see a flash of light through the trees near the bottom of the incline. I can make out a narrow valley and a frozen river winding through thick pines.

I shift to the right and it comes again, a strong pulse of orange before the wind sends branches bobbing up and down, making the light flicker. It looks like a porch light or an outside light, which means that someone lives down there. Someone with a phone who will be able to call for help for Hank, which I will be able to reach a heck of a lot faster than I'll be able to get up to the road, along the highway, and down the drive to the lodge.

Chest hitching with relief, I start down the hill, grateful for the aid of gravity as I gain momentum through the snow. My head doesn't hurt as badly as it did when I woke up, but my thoughts are still sluggish and tangled. Chances are good that I'm in the early stages of hypothermia. If I don't get my body temperature headed back in the right direction soon, I'm going to be in trouble. I have to get to that house and get inside. And if no one's home, then I'll have to break a window and climb in. I don't have much time left, and neither does Hank.

I stumble faster, reaching out to brace myself on tree trunks as I move into the woods, my gaze fixed on the light. I'm getting closer. Almost there, almost there, and it's all going to be okay. I'm going to fix this. I'm going to get Hank help and get back to Nate and tell him about the dream I had and ask him if being dyslexic really makes it harder for him to proofread his books.

"Should hire someone to help," I mumble to the snow-muffled forest. "Or the publisher should. What kind of publisher doesn't have a proofreader on staff?"

I'm growing increasingly outraged by the thought of proofreaders being left out of the publishing process, and also increasingly irritated with my feet, which are not moving nearly as fast as I would like for them to, when something vibrates next to my hip.

My arms fly out to my sides as the buzzing comes again. *Buzz, buzz, buzz, buzz, buzz,* likes someone's in the middle of a texting frenzy.

A texting frenzy!

"Oh my God! Phone!" I shout aloud, fumbling for the zipper on the pocket of my coat. My phone is in my pocket! "Oh thank God. Thank

God!"

I can call for help! Hank and I are going to be okay!

I tug my cell out as I continue to move toward the light, some rational part of me insisting that I still need to get inside that house or I might freeze to death. I swipe right and punch in my code, ignoring the texts continuing to pop up from a number I don't recognize. I don't have time to text, and thanks to the extreme crappiness of my ancient phone, it looks like my battery is about to die.

I dial 911 and hit send, waiting until the voice on the end of the line asks, "What's your emergency," to shout, "My cab driver and I went off the road not far from Tomahawk Mountain House. We were headed into New Paltz and got knocked off the highway. He's passed out behind the wheel and could be dying. You need to send help right away."

"Can you give me your name, ma'am?"

"Did you hear me?" I ask, voice rising. "There's a man named Hank passed out behind the wheel. I put a blanket on him before I got out of the truck, but—"

"I heard you, ma'am, and help is on the way," the woman patiently cuts in. "Can you tell me where you are now? And give me your name so I can relay that to the officers?"

"Oh, I'm, um…" My brain prickles as it tries to think, making me start shivering all over again.

This isn't good. This isn't good at all. "I'm Addie. Addie Klein," I say, my breath coming faster as I realize how close I was to forgetting my own name. I hurry forward, knowing I need to get where I'm going ASAP. "I think I may have a head injury. Or hypothermia. I'm having trouble thinking straight."

"Can you get back inside the truck and warm up, ma'am? Is it safe?"

"Um, I think so…" My words trail off as I spin to look back up the mountain, but I can't see the truck anymore. "I don't know where the truck is. I know it's uphill, but I'm not sure where. I was going to a house to call for help when I realized my phone was in my pocket." I turn back, searching the near darkness under the trees, heart thudding desperately as I realize what else I can't see. "Now I can't see the light, either. I can't see the light from the house!"

"Stay on…line…searching…" The kind voice cuts in and out, increasing the panic building in my chest. "Where….this…okay?"

"I can't hear you," I sob, the tears rising in my eyes going cold almost immediately. "I can't hear you, and I don't know if I can find the truck."

"Location…" The voice turns to static. I thrust the phone overhead, hoping it will strengthen the signal. But when I bring it back to my ear, there's nothing but silence.

"Shit." I glance down at the screen. Call dropped.

I swallow hard, glancing uphill and then downhill, not knowing what to do next. Do I go back up the hill and try to get a signal? Find the truck? Follow the sounds of sirens and hope someone sees my flashlight and comes to get me?

Or do I go downhill and hope I—

Suddenly the orange light flickers on again, maybe fifty feet from where I'm standing. I hurry toward it, determined to reach the house before it goes out again. I lunge forward, stumbling on stiff legs, pulse fast and fluttery. My heart is working hard, but there's only so much one heart can do.

Maybe if you'd had more hearts, you would have been okay.

Or maybe if Eloise had been kinder, or if you'd met Shane sooner, or if Nate had come back into your life before it was too late. But there's only so much one heart can do on its own. It's all right, Adeline. You're tried. The inner voice soothes me as we reach the clearing around the building and realize our mistake. *It's okay to rest. It's okay to sit down and close your eyes for a little while.*

"No," I sob.

What I thought was a house looks like an old trapper's cabin that hasn't been inhabited in decades, and judging by the gaps in the walls, it probably isn't the coziest place to seek refuge. But it doesn't matter. It has to be at least a little warmer in there, and that's what I need. To get warm.

Get inside, get warm, and try to call for help

again.

It's not much of a plan, but it's all my cold-and-injury-fogged brain can manage at the moment.

I slog my way up the snow-covered steps, which thankfully seem sturdier than they look, to the primitive wooden door. I wrap my gloved hand around the handle and pull, expecting to encounter resistance, but the door opens easily, dumping snow onto my arm as it swings on its hinges.

I glance up as I brush off the flakes. The light I've been following must have been from the antique lantern hanging on a hook near the door, but it's out now. Something seems strange about that—about this cabin, too, but I can't focus for long on anything except *get inside, warm up, call again, inside, warm up, call again.*

Dismissing the lantern as a thing I don't have the brainpower for at the moment, I shine my flashlight into the cabin. But as I step inside, the beam stutters, fading to a thin yellow.

I'm jiggling it up and down, trying to get the juice flowing again, when the door slams shut behind me, plunging me into darkness.

Chapter TWENTY

Nate

Fate hasn't given up on Addie and me after all.

If Eduardo hadn't wanted to change our Valentine's Day reservations, or if I'd let him call the concierge instead of coming down in person, then I would have no idea that Adeline was missing.

But I'm not really surprised that I'm in the right place at the right time.

The only thing I feel when the clearly distraught woman behind the concierge desk says—"Tell Hank I'm fine to drive, and I'll meet him at the hospital. And what about Adeline, the woman he was driving to town? Is she okay?"—is a cold rush of dread and the absolute certainty that Adeline is *not* okay.

It's the same thing I've been feeling for the past hour—this nagging, creeping certainty that

Addie is in trouble and that I have to get to her as soon as humanly possible. I move around the two people in line in front of me and lean over the desk, ignoring a dirty look from a man in a snowflake sweater as I slip between him and the concierge.

The petite woman with the white hair glances up at me, pain clear in her eyes as she says into the phone, "Oh no. Please let me know as soon as she's found." She turns her back to me, but I can still hear her. "I should never have let her go out in this storm. If she's hurt, I'll never forgive myself." She pauses, nodding as she listens. "Yes, of course. I'll talk to my manager. I'm sure we can spare people to come help. I'll call you right back, Steven."

She ends the call and turns back to the line at her desk, clearly intending to tell us all that there's been an emergency and we need to take our concerns about dinner and entertainment elsewhere, but I cut her off before she can speak. "Adeline is my friend. What's happened? Where is she?"

"Oh, no. I'm so sorry. There's been an accident," the woman says, pressing her cell phone to her chest with a trembling hand. "My husband was giving her a ride to town when his truck was hit by a drunk driver. It went off the road around the corner from the lodge. Hank's on the way to the hospital, but Adeline wasn't in the truck when the paramedics arrived."

"Where was she?" I ask, my heart clawing its way into my throat.

"No one knows. Apparently she made the call for help," the woman continues, her eyes shining, "but she didn't know where she was at the time. My friend Steven said she sounded confused and might be suffering from hypothermia. The police are searching the woods now, but they asked me to send some of our staff if we can spare them. Obviously, with the temperature dropping, we have to find her as soon as possible."

"I'm coming with the search party," I say, already backing away from the desk. "I'll be back in five minutes. I've just got to grab my coat."

The woman nods, and I turn and run, sprinting across the lobby. I take the stairs to the sixth floor two at a time. Back in the room, as I change into my ski clothes and snow boots, I fill a sleepy Eduardo in on what's happened. In just a few minutes, I'm outfitted for extreme weather and running back out the door with Eduardo hot on my heels.

"I'm coming, too!" He hurries after me, breath coming faster as he struggles into his coat on the way down the stairs. "The more boots on the ground, the sooner we'll find her."

"You don't have to come, Ed," I say, pushing through the door on the ground floor and jogging toward the lobby. "Really. I don't expect you to put yourself at risk."

"Hush," he says, catching up with me near the

registration desk. "Like I'm going to stay here while that sweet thing is wandering around lost in the woods. I'm coming, and we *will* find her, Nathaniel. Don't doubt it. She can't have gotten far in this storm."

Eduardo scores a free seat on a UTV, while I crowd into the back of a pickup truck with three other men outfitted for blizzard conditions. On the way up the hill, I thank them profusely for helping look for Addie, and they each assure me that we're going to find her, that she's going to be fine, and that everything will be all right. But I can't find any comfort in their words. I won't believe things will be all right until I know that Adeline is safe and whole and wrapped up in a blanket somewhere warm.

This is my fault. If I hadn't pushed so hard, she wouldn't have felt like her only choice was to put her safety at risk to get away from me.

I have to find her and tell her that I'll back off, that I won't push, that I'll do whatever she wants me to do as long as she promises to keep herself safe. I don't want to imagine a world without Addie in it. I need her to be alive and happy, even if she decides what will make her happiest is being far away from me.

The thought of never seeing her again hurts like hell, but I'll live through it. I can get through anything as long as I know that Addie's still in the world.

The pickup truck pulls to the side of the road

behind a row of police cars and a small ambulance with its lights spinning and engine running. It's prepped and ready to give Adeline medical attention ASAP.

Now all we have to do is find her.

I'm given a flashlight, a walkie-talkie, a portion of the hillside to search, and strict instructions to check in on schedule. Just a few minutes after hopping from the truck bed, I'm heading down the hill in the darkness, snow stinging into my eyes.

The sun is gone, the clouds are too thick for moonlight to shine through, and by the time I'm fifty feet from the road, the mountain ahead of me is pitch black. The fiercely swirling snow ensures that I can't see more than five feet in front of me, and the wind snatches Addie's name from my lips as soon as I shout it.

By the time I call for my first check-in, my voice is hoarse.

One by one, the other volunteers check in, too, but none of them have found any sign of Adeline or any trail she might have left behind. I try not to let the news gut me—with the snow coming down as hard as it is, any prints she left would have been covered in minutes—but by the time I reach the line where the trees begin to grow closer together, my stomach is in knots and the dread that's been building in my chest has ballooned to fill my entire body.

I feel like I'm trapped in a car spinning on the

ice, fully aware that something terrible is about to happen, but powerless to do anything about it. Addie might already be suffering from extreme hypothermia. If she isn't found soon, it's going to be too late. Another ten, twenty minutes, and I might be finding her body, not the living, breathing woman I love.

And I do love her. I never stopped loving her, and I never will.

"Please, Einstein," I beg as I move deeper into the trees, swallowing hard. "Please be okay. Please hear me and help me find you."

I call her name again and again, hope stretching thinner with every step. Time is ticking by so fast. I'm almost due for my second check-in, which means Adeline's been out here almost an hour and a half.

It's too long. It's too damned long, and my chest feels like someone beat the shit out of me, because I know it. I know it's time to stop hoping for the best and start begging for a miracle.

"Adeline!" I cry out, my voice breaking, her name as close to a prayer as anything else I've got. I wasn't raised with religion, and I've never seen any reason to find some. But as I weave through the trees, I promise the universe I'll find something to believe in, to say thanks to, if it will just take me to Addie before it's too late.

I'm pulling my walkie-talkie out for check-in number two when I see a light flickering through the trees. I hold my breath. After a moment, the light comes again, an orange glow in the dark. I shove the radio back in my pocket and break into a run.

The EMT who briefed us before we headed into the woods said that Adeline had mentioned heading toward a light during her call. He said there wasn't a record of anyone living on this particular hillside, but to keep an eye out just in case.

When the small cabin comes into view I almost choke on my relief. Addie's inside, I know it. I know it the way I know the sky is blue and the sea is wet and that no other woman will ever own my heart the way she does.

I take the steps to the front door two at a time and reach for the handle.

I rip open the door and hurry inside, only to stop dead, blinking hard as I take in the interior of the seemingly abandoned shack. Instead of the crumbling wreck that I'd expected, the inside of the cabin is cozy and warm, furnished with a thick carpet, a bed in one corner, a long table covered with a checkered tablecloth, and two heavy chairs drawn close to a fireplace where flames crackle in the hearth.

And in one of those chairs sits Adeline, wrapped in a thick quilt, fast asleep.

Definitely asleep, nothing more serious. Her bare shoulder, which peeks out of the quilt on one side, is gently rising and falling, and her damp clothes are spread out in front of the fire to dry.

She must have realized that she had to get out of them in order to get her body temperature to rise faster.

Thank God. She's okay, and I can have her back to the ambulance as soon as someone brings dry clothes for her to change into.

Breath rushing out with relief, I pull my radio from my coat. But before I can call to report Addie found, a rumbling fills the air and the boards beneath my feet begin to shake. I glance back at the door just as a large board nailed into the wall slams down, falling into brackets on either side of the frame. A moment later, a loud *sa-lumph* sounds from outside and the entire cabin jerks as snow shoots in beneath the door and, more disturbingly, from the slim space at the top of it.

Heart racing, I hurry to a shuttered window, pulling the wood panels open to reveal cracked glass and…white. Solid white, like the cabin is sitting inside the belly of a giant snowman. I curse as I bring my hands down hard on the wall on either side of the damaged glass. There must have been an avalanche, and a pretty serious one judging by how hard the cabin jerked when the snow hit. There's snow up to the top of the door, at the very least. It could be even higher, and God only knows how far out it goes. Even if it's only a few feet, the chances of me being able to dig us out with my bare hands are slim to none.

I pull the radio out to call for help, but when I

press the transmit button, there's no static, no green light. The damned thing is dead. I reach for my phone, only to find the No Service alert in the upper left hand side of the screen, and I curse again.

"Is it you? Are you really here?" a soft voice asks.

I spin to see Addie standing behind me, her bare feet peeking out of the blue quilt wrapped around her. "I'm here," I hurry across the room to pull her into my arms, hugging her tight. "I'm so glad you're all right."

She presses her face to my chest and inhales. "Oh, I wish I could believe you. You feel so good, but I've been talking to you all night and I'm pretty sure this place isn't real. I think that I'm dreaming it." She pauses before adding in a softer voice, "That I'm dying while I'm dreaming it."

I pull back, cupping her face in my hands and bending down to look her in the eyes. "You're not dying, Addie. And this isn't a dream. I'm really here, but I think we're trapped. There was an avalanche a few minutes ago, and it blocked off the window and the doors."

"Okay." She smiles. "I like the dream where I'm trapped in a cabin with you better than the one where I'm trapped under the water. I especially like that my dream self already had the sense to take her clothes off."

Before I can respond, Addie releases her hold

on the blanket. It falls to the floor, revealing the stunning woman beneath, and I completely forget what I was going to say. I'm too lost in the beauty of her bare breasts, the gentle curve of her belly, the small thatch of hair between her legs, and all her glorious bare skin.

I'm hard before I can talk sense into my cock, and then Addie is in my arms, pressing her lips to mine as she says, "I love you. I could never stop, no matter how hard I tried."

"I love you, too, Ad," I say. "Always have, always will."

"Then make love to me. Please," she whispers, and I forget about the broken radio and the lack of cell service and the fact that Addie and I are buried alive until someone figures out where we are. All I can think about is the woman in my arms and how much I love her and how desperately I need to show her the way she makes me feel.

I scoop her up in my arms and aim us both toward the bed in the corner, where I intend to make love to her until she knows without a shadow of a doubt that she is the only thing that matters, and the only thing I don't ever want to live without.

Chapter
TWENTY-ONE

Addie

Nate lays me down on the bed, and I swear I can feel the scratch of a rough blanket against my skin, smell the woodsy hay and the musk of damp wool. This dream is even more real than being underwater, or the vision of the magic cabin that came to life all around me, the wheels of time turning backward as I watched a rotting disaster transform into a cozy place to hide from the cold.

When the fireplace had sprung to life, I'd half expected the candlesticks on the mantle to ask if I wanted tea. Instead, I'd remained alone in the quiet, and eventually recovered from the shock enough to realize I was shivering and dripping water on the floor.

And so I'd stripped out of my damp clothes, wrapped up in a soft blue quilt by the fire, and fallen into another dream.

Into *this* dream, where Nate is stripping off his clothes, holding my gaze as he peels and tugs and throws fabric to the floor with rough jerks of his hands that make it clear he can't wait to dispose of everything standing between us. And then he's finally naked and back in my arms. His skin is hot, feverish against mine as he kisses me hard and deep and his cock settles between my legs, making me groan into his mouth.

"Yes," I beg, pressing my center against his burning length. "I want you so much."

"I need to kiss every inch of you," he says, kissing his way down my throat. "You're so beautiful, Addie. I'm so glad you're okay. I never want to lose you again. Never fucking again."

I arch into his touch as he cups my breast, brushing his thumb over where I'm tight. Longing rumbles through me like thunder. Then his lips are there, his tongue swirling around my nipple before his mouth closes and he sucks me deep. He feels so good, so electric and brilliant with his bare skin warm against mine that I can't help catching fire.

I spread my legs as his hands skim up my thighs, silently begging for him to touch me anywhere, everywhere. "It was always like this, wasn't it?"

"Like what, beautiful?" he asks, nipping the soft skin beneath my nipple.

"Scary and intense, but so perfect." My head

falls back. "Like drowning. Drowning and being pulled from the water at the same time."

"I love drowning with you." His fingers tease through where I'm already hot and slick as he moans his appreciation against my breast. "I love how wet you are for me. I can't wait to be inside you, to feel you all around me. I want to get lost in you, Einstein. Forever."

"Yes, please, yes," I beg, threading my fingers through his hair as his mouth moves to my other breast, licking and sucking until I'm writhing against his hand, so close to coming that I'm dizzy with it.

But I don't want to go yet, not without him.

"Not yet," I pant, nails digging into Nate's scalp. "Please. Inside. Now. I need you. I can't wait. Don't make me wait."

"I'll never make you wait, baby." He lifts his mouth from my breast, holding my gaze as he fits the head of his cock to where my body weeps for him. "I promise. Never again."

And then he pushes inside, driving deep, and it hurts.

It *hurts*, sharp and fierce, almost like the first time all those years ago. There's a piercing sting and I gasp, but then Nate's mouth is on mine and he's kissing me the way only he can kiss, dulling my awareness of the pain. He kisses me until I know that I am beautiful, special, irreplaceable. Until his love soaks through my skin and my blood rushes faster and the pain bleeds into pleasure.

Pure, mind-blowing pleasure.

"Perfect," I gasp against his lips. "It's so perfect."

"You're so beautiful, Addie. I love you so much." He advances and retreats, gliding in and out, stoking the fire he's built as our tongues dance together in an endless, dizzying, time-bending kiss. I wrap my legs tighter around his hips and lift into his thrusts, silently begging for more of him, all of him.

"Take me." My fingers dig into the strong muscles of his back, his ass, drawing him deeper, closer. "Take me, Nate. I want you to come. Come with me."

"Not yet." His voice is tight as he shifts the angle of our connection until he's rubbing against the top of my sex at the end of every thrust. "I need more. I need forever with you. Just like this."

"Yes. Just like this."

"Just you and me, Ad." He brushes his thumb across my nipple in time to his thrusts, building the tension swelling impossibly large inside of me.

I bite my lip, fighting to keep from finding home without him, but it's too late and I'm too far gone. "I'm coming. I can't stop. Oh God, I can't stop!"

"Don't stop. Come, baby." A pained expression twists his features. "Fuck, Adeline, yes, come for me. I love feeling you come."

"With me," I demand, holding on tight as he rides me harder, faster. "Come with me, please. Please!"

He cries out, his arm wrapping tight around my waist as his rhythm grows wild, frantic. I urge him on, rushing to meet him as a second wave builds inside of me.

Faster, harder, tighter, deeper, we strain together, stormy and breathless until finally we collide.

I call his name as pleasure rushes over me, knocking me down and dragging me under. And suddenly I'm drowning again, but this time it's not cold. It's sweet fire licking through my bones, burning my skin, making my nerve endings sizzle, filling me with so much bliss that I have no choice but to open my mouth and scream, simply to give the beauty a place to go.

I cry out as my orgasm spirals on and on, until there isn't a drop of life left in me, until my soul is naked in the cool air, pulsing between our bodies as Nate pulls out and comes, his cock jerking hard against my belly.

"Addie," he groans, his jaw clenched tight. "Oh God, it hurts. It's so good it hurts."

I moan my agreement as my arms go around him, holding his sweat-damp body close, relishing the feeling of his heart thundering against my chest. He feels so real. So warm and safe and perfect. I haven't thought much about the afterlife lately—not since I realized that the church of my childhood and I were never going to see eye to eye—but if this is heaven, I'll take it.

"Or maybe it's purgatory," I mumble, fingers skimming up and down Nate's muscled back. "And sex is the way we'll purify our souls."

"What's that?" He pulls back, gazing down at me with a confused smile.

"I was thinking that maybe this is purgatory, not heaven. And making love is the way we'll atone for our sins." I arch a weary brow. "Or how I'll atone for mine since you're not really here."

A troubled look creeps into his eyes. "Adeline, I *am* here. I promise. I came from the hotel with the search party that's looking for you right now. Someone could be here to help us any second."

I nod patiently. "Yes, you said that before. But this room isn't real and neither are you. I saw it transform. Right in front of me. Like special effects in a movie, but real." I frown. "But *not* real. You know what I'm saying?"

"You were probably hallucinating from being out in the cold too long, baby." He curses softly as he rolls off of me, reaching down to pluck his boxers off the floor. "And now I've taken advantage of you while you're out of your head."

"No, you haven't." I prop up on my elbows. "I'm thinking perfectly straight. I know what I saw. I wasn't hallucinating. One minute, this place was a dump falling in on itself, and the next it was like a magic clock had turned back time. I saw it.

Really. And I talked to you while I was dreaming in the truck, before I woke up the first time. You told me about being dyslexic."

"You already knew I was dyslexic."

"Yes, but I didn't know it made it hard for you to proofread your books," I say, not encouraged by his long sigh in response. "Are you trying to tell me I'm crazy? That it doesn't make it harder to proof your books?"

"No, it does, but…" He turns back to me, his gaze fixed on my knees. "Let's get you dressed and then we can talk some more, okay? I don't want you to get cold again."

I frown harder, starting to wonder if maybe I did get confused at some point. But before I can remember why this being real is a bad thing, Nate draws his boxers across my stomach, wiping away the stickiness, revealing the scar between my hips.

"What's that, Addie?" he asks, brows furrowing.

"Nothing." I sit up fast, pulling my knees to my chest. But it's already too late.

"It's not nothing," The shock in his eyes as he watches me scoot to the far side of the bed makes my guts twist. "Is that what I think it is?"

"I don't want to talk about it." I hug my legs tighter. "I want my clothes."

"I'll get your clothes." He moves closer, worry in his tone. "But that looks a hell of a lot like a C-section scar. Is that what it is?"

I bite my lip, squeezing my eyes shut.

"Jesus, Addie, if we have a baby out there somewhere, you've got to tell me. Is that what happened?" he says, pushing on when I refuse to answer. "You were pregnant and your mom found out? That's it, isn't it? That's why she made you leave town and drop out of college? Fuck, I'm so stupid."

I shake my head as I whisper, "I don't talk about it."

"Well, you're going to have to talk about it." His voice is gentle, but firm. "At least once, because I need to know the truth. Is this why you can't talk to me? Because of this? Because I've got a son or daughter out there, and you didn't tell me?"

The words flick a switch deep inside of me, setting the monster I've kept under wraps for so long free to roar toward the surface.

And roar it does.

One second I'm cowering in the corner, trembling, the next my mouth opens and all the rage, hurt, and heartbreak comes rushing out, claws bared, aimed right at Nate.

Chapter TWENTY-TWO

Nate

"I didn't tell you?" Her voice is soft, but her eyes are glittering with a sudden rage that makes it clear I've said the wrong fucking thing. "How was I supposed to *tell you*, when you were *gone*? How was I supposed to tell you that the morning-after pill didn't work when you'd left me to deal with the test and my mother and being pregnant all by myself? At sixteen, when I was practically still a child?"

"I'm sorry. That didn't come out right. That's not what I meant." I reach for her, only to have her slap my hand away.

I pull back, surprised by how much it stings. But then, I was always the one who said Addie was stronger than anyone gave her credit for.

Though I had no idea how strong, or how much she's been through.

"I'm sorry, baby," I say. "I'm—"

"No. You don't get to touch me, or call me baby." She presses closer to the wall, legs still hugged to her chest. "And you don't get to tell me what I have to talk about, either. That baby was *mine*. It was never yours because you were never there. I was there, all by myself, in a halfway house for girls who had shamed their Catholic families, and no one ever came to visit. Not even my mom or dad."

She pulls in a breath, her eyes shining brighter. "And I was so miserable that nothing could make it better. Nothing. Not even books, because I couldn't read without thinking of you and wondering what you would say about the story." Her teeth dig into her lip. "You were that deep in my head. And like the dumb kid I was, I kept thinking that you were going to show up. That leaving had been some terrible misunderstanding, and that—"

"It was, Addie. You know—"

"And that you were going to ride up to the house on a white horse," she says, raising her voice to drown out my excuses, "tell me you loved me, and take me away from all the sad, ugly shit. But you never did." She blinks, sending tears streaming down her cheeks. "You never did, and when I went into labor too early for the baby to live, I was still alone so the housemother took me to St. Mary's. After I was there a few hours, I started bleeding so badly they had to give me a blood transfusion, but everyone acted like there was nothing else they could do. For me, or for the baby."

"God, Addie," I say, my heart breaking for her.

"We all knew she was going to die," she continues in a softer voice. "And that maybe I would die, too, but the doctors' hands were tied. There are no abortions allowed in Catholic hospitals, even in cases like mine, when the baby has no chance and the mother is getting sicker every day."

She swallows hard, her lips curving in a sad smile. "I was so scared that I was actually glad to see my mother when she showed up. I thought she would help me, make it better with a kiss the way she did when I was little." Her smile fades. "She'd only been there a few minutes when one of the nurses, who had been especially good to me, pulled Mom aside and hinted strongly that I should be taken to another hospital where I could be treated more effectively. But Mom said I had to stay. That it was God's will."

I reach for her again, but she holds a hand up between us.

"By the time my father finally took me to another hospital, against Mom's wishes, I was out of my mind with fever and had been miscarrying for days. The baby only lived a few minutes, but I didn't get to see her. The bleeding had started again and the doctors were busy cutting me open to see if they could get it stopped before I died, too."

Her breath escapes in a long, tired sigh. "And that's why I have a scar. And why I didn't make it to college. Mom told Dad she would leave him and take the boys if he tried to bring me home. So Dad found me a job working as a live-in companion to a friend of the family, an old woman who for years treated me like a puppet to be jerked around for her entertainment. But for the longest time, I didn't even *think* about standing up to her. I thought that's what I deserved, Nate. That I deserved to be unloved and alone and living one day to the next without daring to hope for anything more."

"Adeline." Her name is a plea for her to stop and let me comfort her—let me tell her that she's worth a hundred of her father and a thousand of her crazy, abusive mother—but she doesn't.

"Why would I have assumed otherwise?" She laughs as she mops the tears from her cheeks with both hands. "Everyone I've ever loved has decided that I'm not worth the time or the energy. You know I'm a fan of the scientific method. With experiment results like that, what other logical conclusion could I have drawn? Honestly, if Shane hadn't come into my life and been such an amazing friend to me, I don't know if I ever would have worked up the courage to hope again. Sometimes all it takes is the kindness of one person, but until that one person comes along…"

"You are the most lovable person I've ever met, Adeline Klein," I say, my voice thick with emotion. Everything she went through, not just without me but *because of me*, makes my chest feel like it's collapsing. "And I'm so sorry. So sorry I don't have words for it. I know that isn't good enough, but—"

"No, it isn't." Her gaze falls to the mattress as she shakes her head loosely from side to side. "It isn't good enough. And now we've done it again."

"Done what?"

"Made the same mistake," she says, her voice distant. "The same mistake, over and over, trapped in a terrible circle with nothing but pain to show for it."

I realize she must be talking about having sex without a condom, which I sure as hell wouldn't have risked if I'd known what I know now, and hurry to assure her, "I pulled out, Addie. We'll be fine. And if we're not, I'll be right there with you. You're never going to go through something like that alone again. I promise."

"It's too late." She shakes her head again, her gaze fixed on some faraway memory only she can see. "You can't change the past."

"But we can change the future." I lean closer, wrapping gentle fingers around her ankle. "Will you look at me Addie? Please? We can make things better. We can have the future. Together. You and me."

"There is no future," she whispers. "Everything has already happened. You know that. You remember how this works."

Cold air seeps in through the thin walls, making me shiver. "You're not making sense, Einstein. We need to get you dressed and warmed up. I shouldn't have let you get cold again. This is my fault."

"I'm not cold." Her head cants to the side and her brows lift.

If I didn't know better, I would swear that she's listening to someone whispering in her ear. Even worse, I would almost say that I can hear the voice, too—a soft, lulling whisper assuring us both that this is the way it goes. These are the parts we play, no point in resisting.

Might as well rage at the sun while it sets. No matter how loud we scream, or how hard we fight, the light is sliding away and there's nothing we can do to hold on to it. It's already slipped through our fingers a hundred times before.

"Not cold. Not hot. I don't feel much of anything anymore, really," Addie mumbles as she rises, padding naked across the room, her shadow moving with her.

At first, I only notice that the shadow looks strange, but then Addie turns to face the fire and I realize what's so wrong about the dark form. The shadow is *in front* of her, not behind, the way it should be. The only light in the room comes from the fireplace and the candles on the mantle.

Adeline's face should be bathed in yellow and gold, but I can barely make out her features. The shadow is blocking the flickering light because it's taller than Addie, too. Taller and broader through the shoulders, with long, straight hair that falls almost to the ground as it looks up at the shotgun mounted over the fireplace.

A shotgun that I would bet my hands wasn't there when I stepped into the cabin.

And suddenly I'm no longer Nate Casey who loves Addie and is insanely worried about her. I'm Nate West, author of ghost stories and collector of unexplained things. I'm back in those endless hours I spent at that castle in northern Scotland, huddled in a ball on the floor, shaking and sweating because I was so tempted to hurt myself that I was afraid to stand up.

I'd never had a suicidal thought before that night and haven't had one since, but in those never-ending hours, I came so close to ending things that it still shakes me just to think about it. I nearly killed myself that night, just like the man who had been hired to look after the castle before me, the woman who'd bought the property after it stood vacant for a century, and the original owner, a lord who had cut his throat to avoid being hanged for murdering his wife and child, when it became clear he wasn't the baby's father.

I've never seen anything like this shadow now, but I know there are things in this world that can't be explained. I know that we are all haunted by our own monsters, and that sometimes those things are strong enough to live on after the people they torment are gone. Sometimes they leave scars on the next generation, the way our parents' demons have left scars on Addie and me.

And sometimes pain cuts so deep that it leaves claw marks in time and space, shredded, ugly, stuck places that defy the natural order. Places almost everyone can sense are wrong if they take the time to stop and smell the air. Those are the places that become the inspiration for ghost stories—the woods that travelers are afraid to pass through after dark, the haunted houses where bad things keep happening no matter how many times a property changes hands.

My skin goes cold, crawling with the certainty that Addie and I need to get out of this cabin as fast as fucking possible.

"Adeline, why don't you put your clothes on," I say in a mild voice, not wanting to attract the attention of the shadow. "And let's see if we can get through the snow in front of the door. The rescue team isn't far."

"That's not how it happens," Addie says. "It starts here. By the fire."

"What starts?" The hairs at the back of my neck rise as something moves in the darkness by the table on the other side of the room. Another shadow, this one so large its head nearly touches the ceiling.

"You have the knife." Her pale hand lifts,

pointing at the other shadow and then at the mantle. "And then I have the gun."

My gut clenches. The ghost story Mitch told me. Why didn't I pay closer attention? Haven't I learned by now that nothing, no matter how small, can be taken for granted?

"And then I try to get out. *After*, not before," Addie says dreamily. She's clearly caught up in a story that isn't ours, but our story has power, too. I need to remind Addie of that before what happened in this cabin plays out all over again.

"Look at me Addie." I step into my pants, wanting to be dressed and ready to haul ass as soon as I bring her back to me. "There isn't going to be a knife or a gun. Things are different now."

"Nothing's different." She sways closer to the fire. "And I'm tired of broken promises."

"What promises did I break, Einstein? Do you remember?" I move closer, needing to be within tackling distance if Addie—or whatever else is in here with us—decides to go for the gun. "Can you tell me?"

"You said you wouldn't go away, but you did. I had to cut the firewood myself. And when the men building the hotel came, there was no one here to protect me." She sniffs, her voice breaking. "I was all alone."

A man who went away and a woman alone, one who endured incredible pain. It's no surprise Addie's been sucked into this other woman's story, but there arc ways that our story is different, and the faster I can get her focused on those the better.

"You weren't alive when the hotel was being built, Addie. The hotel opened over a hundred years ago. You weren't even born."

She glances my way, her expression wavering between anger and uncertainty. "I know what happened. You left!"

"I left seven years ago, when we were both kids." I take another small step forward. "We never had the chance to live together, and if we had, I wouldn't have left you alone. I would have cut all the wood and spent the winter tucked into bed right beside you, keeping you warm and showing you how much I love you."

Her tongue worries the corner of her mouth as she shakes her head. "No, I remember what happened. I have callouses on my hands from the axe." She lifts her hands, staring at her palms, blinking faster. "Wh-where did they go?"

"Do you remember the day we met?" I take advantage of her distraction to close the last of the distance between us. "What were the chances that we would both be reading the same old horror novel? And that we would both go down to the middle of nowhere, New Jersey, to visit the hellmouth on the same day at the exact same time?"

"We…" She frowns, then slowly nods. "We lived in different towns, in different states. If we hadn't picked up that book…"

"We might never have met," I say at the same time that she does, making her eyes go wide and her lips twitch at the edges

"Yes," she says, her sudden smile fading. "I used to think that meant something."

"It does mean something." I hold her gaze, refusing to look at the shadow shifting restlessly near the fire, or the other shadow prowling back and forth beside the table, getting bigger and darker with every minute that passes. "Just like it means something that Eduardo and I were the first people to drive by after your car broke down, and that we both booked rooms at Tomahawk on the same weekend, and that of all the millions of people in New York we're two of the very few who know a guy who runs a secret get-revenge-on-your-ex service." I funnel every bit of my belief that Addie and I are meant to be into my voice. "The universe is trying to send us a message Adeline. Our story isn't finished yet, not by a long shot."

"Message! My phone!" She points to the floor where her clothes are spread out to dry, her voice growing more focused. "I was reading a text message from your friend Mitch before I fell asleep. The pervert who texted me from Paris is your friend! What are the odds of that?"

I'm about to assure her "zero to fucking none," when she looks down and her arms fly to cover her chest. "Oh my God, I'm still naked." She turns, casting a horrified glance at me over her shoulder. "Don't look! I need to get dressed."

"I've already seen it all, babe. And you're beautiful," I say, too scared to take my eyes off of her for a second. I can't risk losing her again. "But you should definitely get dressed. Get dressed, and then we're going to get out of here, even if we have to dig our way through an avalanche to do it."

Addie nods as she steps into her panties and reaches for her bra, fear creeping in to tighten her features. "I think you're right. And I think maybe we were wrong before."

"Wrong about what?" I keep my attention fixed on her as I hustle back into the rest of my clothes. The shadows are growing progressively agitated, pacing and rippling and raising their arms overhead, clearly determined to play out their story whether Addie and I cooperate or not.

Her throat works as she wraps her scarf around her neck and shrugs her coat on. "Maybe this is closer to a dream than you thought."

"Agreed." My pulse spikes as I tug on my boots and the shadow closest to Addie throws her head back in a long, silent scream. For a moment I'm tempted to ask Ad if she can see the silhouette, but decide against drawing her attention to anything that might pull her back into that other story.

"Well, I don't know about you, but I'm ready to wake up." Addie crosses the room and takes my hand, holding on tight. "Let's get the hell out of here."

"Right fucking now," I agree, heading for the door. Addie and I are steps away from the exit when the radio in my pocket lets out a loud, angry squawk.

I curse, fumbling for the walkie-talkie, but before I can pull it out, a woman's scream erupts from the speaker. It's so loud that Addie and I both cry out in surprise, our hands flying to cover our ears. The second our gloved hands part, the lights go out, plunging the cabin into darkness as the air fills with loud, angry voices.

Chapter
TWENTY-THREE

Addie

I am an ordinary woman who has lived an ordinary life.

Or at least that's the story I've told myself the past seven years, as I've done my best to forget the magical boy I met one summer and all the incredible things we discovered while we were reading and talking and making love and stealing away for adventures and falling so hard for each other there was a time when Nate felt like a part of me.

But there are some things—strange, extraordinary things—that you never completely leave behind, no matter how ordinary your life becomes. You can shove them deep down into your subconscious and tuck them behind a wall of boxes filled with things you prefer not to acknowledge with your waking mind, but all it takes is a whiff of memory to bring them rushing back to the surface with the speed of a bullet train.

As the room goes black and a woman's scream fills the air, followed by the howl of a man demanding, "Tell me what you did! Tell me what you did, you fucking whore," I'm sucked back to the summer before I turned seventeen. I'm back in the woods where Nate and I were lost for hours before we stumbled upon a shack where I mistakenly thought we might find help.

But instead we heard screaming. Screaming voices raging in the dark.

"We have to get out of here!" I try to reach for Nate in the darkness, but my arm is limp and weak, refusing to move. I'm inside myself and outside myself at the same time. A part of me is here in the shadows, with the winter wind howling outside and the screams of the woman begging for her lover to "let me go! Let me go!"

The other part of me is reaching for a rock in another time and place, where the summer sun is setting. She's turning to Nate and saying, "Do it, please. We have to do something and you can throw harder than I can," and watching as he takes the stone, pulls back his arm, and—

The sound of shattering glass fills the air as the rock breaks through the window, bringing light crashing into the room along with it.

I spin, smelling evergreens in summer as I catch a glimpse of the world outside through a hole in the muddy glass. I see a boy with broad shoulders and a girl with wild curly hair turning to run away through sunlit woods just as Nate screams, "Adeline!"

Outside, the girl turns, glancing over her shoulder with a shocked expression.

And from the darkness inside a cabin buried in the snow, I have the not-at-all-ordinary experience of staring through a summer's day into my own eyes.

My sixteen-year-old eyes.

The eyes of the girl who has no idea what the next seven years are going to hold for her, but who wouldn't be afraid if she did. She isn't afraid because she knows that she is loved and strong and where she's supposed to be, with the boy who is so exactly what she needs that there is no doubt in her mind that he was made just for her. I watch as the boy—Nate before he finished becoming a man—turns back for the girl, wrapping his arm around her waist and half-carrying her along the trail because there is no way that he would run for safety without her.

"Jesus. Are you seeing what I'm seeing?" Nate's voice is a choked whisper, but I can hear him.

The screams are gone.

I take his hand, holding tight as the light streaming in from the window winks out. And then the air is cold again and we're alone in a building so old and run down that snow puffs in through the gaps in the walls and the next strong wind could level the structure flat.

"Outside. Now," Nate says.

The boards beneath my feet groan as he guides me across the room and rips open the door. We hurry down the stairs, which are no longer covered by an avalanche that happened over a hundred years ago, and cross the clearing without looking back.

"We'll talk about all of that later." He squeezes my hand tight, making it clear he has no intention of letting go.

"Later," I agree, following him up the hill. The storm isn't as bad as it was before. Enough moonlight filters through the clouds for us to make our way through the trees without a flashlight, which is good since we left both of our flashlights in the ghost house.

"But you saw it, right?" he asks, breath rushing out. "Saw…us?"

"Yes. Us. That day we were lost in the woods."

"That's fucking insane, Ad." He shakes his head. "That isn't possible."

"'There are more things in heaven and earth, Horatio, than are dreamt of in your philosophy,'" I quote, though I'm inclined to agree with him.

"'Though this be madness, yet there is method in't,'" he quotes back.

"A method seems likely. I certainly don't know anyone else who has as much of Hamlet memorized as we do."

"But those aren't my favorite lines." He stops, turning to grip me by the upper arms as we reach the edge of the tree line. "'Doubt thou the stars are fire; Doubt that the sun doth move; Doubt truth to be a liar; But never doubt I love.'" He curls a gloved hand around the back of my neck, pulling me closer. "That one always makes me think of you."

"Me too," I whisper. "Of you."

"I'm sorry, Adeline." His breath is warm on my lips, but it's something less tangible that sends a wave of comfort rushing through me. "I'm sorry I let you down and left you alone. I'm sorry you went through hell and I wasn't there to at least hold your hand."

"It isn't your fault. But I'm glad you know. I should have told you before, but…" I shake my head. "I just didn't know how. For years, I refused to even think about that time in my life. I thought ignoring it and pushing it away made the ugliness easier to live with, but it didn't. It made it so strong I wasn't sure I could handle letting the truth out of its cage. Does that make any sense?"

"It makes all the sense." He wraps his arms around me, hugging me tight. "Stories are powerful. They can also be poisonous, especially if you've got no one to share them with. Sharing dilutes the hard stuff, makes it bearable, you know?"

I sigh. "Makes sense."

"But you don't have to carry any of this alone anymore," he promises. "I'm here, and I'm not going anywhere."

"I know." An unexpected laugh bubbles up from deep inside me. "Even if you tried, I have a feeling something would bring you back."

"Right?" He casts a narrow glance back the way we came.

"You realize we might have the creepiest love story ever."

"Good." He smiles. "Seems fitting, considering the way we met, don't you think?"

"I suppose so." I wrap my arms around his waist, grunting as something hard digs into my ribs. "What is that? You got a brick in your pocket?"

"No, I'm just happy to see you," he says, making me laugh again, though a few minutes ago I was sure laughter had left the building. "It's my walkie-talkie. We're probably close enough to call the search party and let them know we're on our way back to the road."

"Yes! Call them!" I pull away, making shooing motions with my hands to hurry him along. "The sooner people know we're coming, the sooner I'm going to believe we're actually getting out of these woods alive."

"We're getting out alive." He pulls out the radio. "But what are we going to say happened while we were in the woods?"

"The truth," I say, without hesitation. "I'm

done with anything that's not the truth. I'm not going to lie to myself or anyone else ever again, and if people think I'm crazy, then that's their right. But it's my right to say that a ghost cabin saved my life." I frown. "And then it almost killed me. And maybe you, too. But we were saved by a rock you threw through a window seven years ago." I press my lips together, nodding as my eyes grow heavy. "Right. I see your point. We'll tell them we were lost in an area where your walkie-talkie wasn't working."

"Sounds good." He presses the transmit button and speaks into the receiver, "This is Nate. I found Adeline. She's okay, and we're on our way back up the mountain. We're at the tree line and should be able to see the road in just a few minutes. Over."

"Thank God!" A relieved male voice crackles through the speaker. "We've got people coming to meet you. So glad she's okay. Over."

"What about Hank?" Worry floods through my chest as my mind regains its grip on reality. "Is he all right?"

"He's on his way to the hospital and is going to be fine. His wife, Francine, helped get the search party together to look for you."

"How did you find out about it? Did they make an announcement at the lodge?"

He shakes his head. "Nope. I was just in the right place at the right time."

"Another crazy coincidence." I lean into him

as his arm comes around my shoulders and we start back up the hill through the snow.

"I don't believe in coincidences anymore. Not when it comes to you and me. It's fate, Einstein. And the sooner we come to terms with that, the sooner we can get on with things."

"Things like what?" I glance up at him as we step out of the woods, close enough to the road to see the swirling lights of a line of the emergency vehicles at the top of the rise.

"Things like being in love and making up for lost time." The hope in his words hits me right in the heart. "I don't want to waste another minute I could be spending with you. You're the only adventure I can't live without, and if you'll give me another chance I promise you won't regret it."

I blink back tears. "I think another chance can be arranged."

"Does that mean you'll be my Valentine tomorrow?" he asks as flashlights cut through the darkness, headed our way. "I've got reservations at the hotel restaurant. Maybe you and I could make it a first date?"

"Sex in a haunted cabin doesn't count as a first date?"

"Making love to you is never something I'm going to regret." He shudders as he hugs me closer. "But the sooner we make some memories to replace getting busy on the ghost mattress, the better."

I hum my agreement. "I wonder if we picked

up ghost bed bugs from the eighteen eighties?"

He shudders. "Or ghost crabs."

"Ew!" I laugh and immediately feel terrible about it. "God, it's not funny, though. People died there. We did it in a crime scene, Nate."

He looks vaguely nauseous. "We didn't know it was a crime scene."

"We knew it was a stranger's bed," I say, waving as Eduardo's cheery face comes into sight beside two policemen in uniform. "Personally, I think there's only one way to make this better."

"Name it," he says.

"You. In my room. Tonight." Before he can answer, Eduardo swoops in, scooping me up in a fierce, papa-bear hug. But that's okay. I don't need an answer. The look on Nate's face makes it clear he'll be in my bed as soon as we can make it back to the lodge and up the stairs. And for that I will count myself a lucky girl, no matter how much bad luck I've had in my life.

"I'm so glad you're okay, darling." Eduardo squeezes me tight to his chest. "I was so worried, and Nathaniel was beside himself." He lowers his voice, adding for my ears only, "He's desperately in love with you, sweet pea. I hope you'll consider giving him another chance. He really does seem to be one of the good ones, and he's so pretty to look at."

"He is both of those things and so much more," I whisper, kissing Ed's scruffy cheek. "Thank you for coming to look for me. Does this mean we're friends? I could really use a few more friends in the city."

"Of course, we're friends, doll!" He puts me down with a laugh, helping a police officer wearing a red scarf wrap a blanket around my shoulders as I assure everyone that I'm fine and can walk to the ambulance on my own.

"I'm honored by the offer of friendship," Eduardo says, falling in between Nate and me. "And as soon as we get back to civilization, we're going to celebrate your survival with a spa day. My treat. We'll gossip and get to know each other and I'll show you how amazing this hair of yours can be with the right cut."

"She doesn't need a new haircut," Nate says from my other side. "She's beautiful the way she is."

"Well, of course she is." Eduardo leans in, adding in a conspiratorial voice. "But there's no shame in letting a friend treat you to a makeover. Especially when that friend is one of the top names in the fashion industry. Stick with me, gorgeous, and we'll have this boy drooling at your feet in no time."

"He's already pretty drooly," I say, as Nate grunts and says, "Very drooly. And not ashamed of it."

I grin at him before turning back to Eduardo. "But I would love to have a spa day. I'm going to be job hunting soon, and a new haircut will boost my confidence during the interviews, if nothing else."

"Job hunting, you say." Eduardo taps a gloved finger to his lips. "Let's talk more tomorrow over coffee, but I know a few people who are hiring. It's mostly entry level, personal assistant type work, but—"

"I would be thrilled with entry level work. I'd be thrilled with just about anything, honestly. But the only job I've ever had was working for an old woman who decided to fire me after I refused to help her get a harmless homeless man put in jail, so I won't have any references."

"Oh, that won't be a problem," Eduardo says with a wave of his hand. "I'll tell them you're adorable, and they'll trust me because I have excellent judgment when it comes to friends. Boyfriends, not so much, but that's a subject for another day, when you haven't been wandering around the woods with hypothermia."

Thankfully, it turns out that I *don't* have hypothermia, and after a brief examination in the back of the ambulance—during which the paramedics marvel that I'm not showing any signs of exposure after being out in the cold for hours, and I shrug and pretend to be confused, too, because talking about ghost cabins would be a good way to get hauled into the psych ward—I'm cleared to head back to the hotel.

Nate and I are given seats inside the pickup truck and delivered safely to the lobby by a very nice man who is clearly relieved that this night has a happy ending.

But not as happy as I am.

"Room number twelve fifteen," I whisper to Nate as we step inside the lobby, where the Valentine's Day tree is looking strangely lovely all of a sudden. "Bring condoms this time?"

"I'll buy out the hotel store and be up in a few minutes," he says, kissing my cheek. "Don't fall asleep before I get there."

I arch a brow. "Do I look tired to you? I'm wired, Casey. You'll be lucky if you sleep at all tonight. I've got seven years of celibacy to make up for."

His smile fades. "Seven years?"

"Only you," I confirm softly. "I was thinking about making an effort to get out and play the field when I got back to the city, but I think I've changed my mind."

"You *think* you've changed your mind?"

"Yes, I think I have." I fight a grin as his eyes narrow in mock anger. "But maybe if you're really good tonight, you can close the deal."

"Oh, I'm going to close the deal." He squeezes my hip, sending a wave of heat through me to pool between my legs. "I'm going to make you come so many times you're going to forget that other cocks exist, Klein. I'm going to give you a raging case of cock-nesia."

I laugh as he pulls me into his arms under the sparkling ornaments of the V-Day tree. "Cock-nesia. That sounds serious. And a raging case?

Will I ever recover?"

"Not if I have anything to say about it," he says, dropping his lips to mine. And then he kisses me breathless right there in the middle of the lobby, while dozens of strangers walk by, going on with their lives oblivious to the miracle that happened tonight.

***

In the months that follow, Nate and I give what we experienced a lot of names—fate, kismet, acid-flashback-even-though-neither-of-us-had-ever-done-acid—but in my heart it's always just the Miracle. The Miracle of Us, of finding what we were certain was lost, and learning there is nothing love can't do.

Truly nothing.

There are more things in heaven and earth than we can dream of, but love's imagination is limitless. Just like my love for this man who was meant for me.

Part THREE

~°~ *And for always...* ~°~

Chapter
TWENTY-FOUR

From the texts of Shane Willoughby Falcone,
Mitch McKibbon, and Adeline Klein

Shane: Are you sure you want to do this?

Addie: Of course I'm sure! It's the perfect
surprise.

Shane: You don't think a cabin in the wilderness
is a little on the nose after the way you two spent
last Valentine's Day eve?

Addie: It's a cabin in the wilderness surrounded
by other cabins, a good hundred miles from the
scary cabin. And the Lover's Leap Lodge isn't
haunted.
I did a thorough background check before I made
reservations.
Nate and I will be fine.

Shane: Lover's Leap?! So the lovers survived the leap...

Mitch: No, they died, but they didn't come back to haunt the joint. I did some checking around, too, just to be safe. As much as I love Nathaniel and Adeline, I don't want to spend my long weekend saving them from ghosts. Eduardo and I are going to be shacking up on the other side of the compound, and we're looking forward to some alone time.

Addie: Aw, I love that you and Eduardo are in love! Isn't he the best?
(Remember that he's my favorite papa bear, Pervert, and if you break his heart I will break your face.)

Mitch: Shane, have you noticed that Addie's violent side is getting more violent lately?

Shane: I have! She's growing up to be just as righteously bitchy as I always hoped she would. *wipes tear* I'm so proud.
And I second that sentiment, Mitchell. Eduardo is lovely and gives the best haircuts in the entire world. If you hurt him, I will also be forced to hurt your face.
Nothing personal.

Mitch: What about MY heart?

Is someone going to break Eddie's face if he decides I'm boring and trades me in for a cuter model with less back fat and a better job? I'm not burning the world down with my writing yet, unlike SOME people.

Addie: Eduardo would never trade you in. He's totally smitten, and you know you're adorable, Mitchell. Especially when you let him dress you up.
Which reminds me, was he able to get the special delivery I asked him about?

Mitch: If you mean the raunchy lingerie I mailed to the hotel yesterday so it will be there waiting for your kinky self when you arrive, then yes, Adeline.
But seriously, gag me. I don't like to imagine you in outfits like that. You're like the sweet, if occasionally violent, little sister I never had.

Addie: I don't like you imagining me in that outfit, either!
You shouldn't have looked in the bag!
Why did you look?!!!

Shane: Ooo, I want to know what's in the bag! Is it crotch-less panties?

Mitch: Ew!
Addie: No!

Shane: A leather corset with cut out nipple holes?

Mitch: EW! STOP!

Addie: I'm not going to tell you what it is. It's private, to help celebrate Nate's book deal for the scary books. Just for Nate and me.

Shane: And Mitch. If Mitch knows, I should know.
I was your friend first, Adeline. I have dibs.

Mitch: Dibs on knowing what kind of BDSM-y lingerie she's wearing on Valentine's Day?

Addie: MITCH!

Shane: BDSM? Oh my…
So are you going to spank him, or is he going to spank you?

Addie: No one is spanking anyone!

Mitch: Well, that doesn't sound like much fun.

Shane: Yeah, somebody should get spanked. Or at least tied up.
I enjoy being tied up, but Jake gets a little claustrophobic, so make sure Nate isn't claustrophobic before you tie him too tight.

Addie: I thought you didn't kiss and tell!

Shane: I don't. I was talking about bondage and spanking, not kissing. ;)
What do you think, Mitch?
Do you think Nate is the claustrophobic type?

Mitch: I'm staying out of it.
I've been trying to get a new nickname for a year.
I'll never stop being Pervert in Paris if I get sucked into this kind of conversation.

Shane: Now who's no fun? :P

Addie: Geez…
Can I just get confirmation that you'll get Nate out of the office, Shane?
And that you'll be downstairs ready to kidnap him, Mitchell?
Then we can all get on with our lives and pretend this over-sharing never happened.

Shane: Yes, ma'am. I will shoo Nate down the stairs before he gets sucked into the poker game, and refrain from telling Bash or Penny anything until after he leaves, since they can rarely be trusted with secrets.

Mitchell: And Eduardo and I will be poised and ready to pounce, and will refuse to tell Mr. Fabulous where he's going until we arrive. Even if he puts up a fight over being kidnapped the day before Valentine's Day.

Addie: He won't. He thinks I'm out of town until Monday.
I told him the final interview was on Sunday instead of today.

Shane: Speaking of the final interview!!
How did it go? Did you get in?!
I've been dying to be nosy, but I didn't want to upset you if the news wasn't good. But now that you've brought it up I can't help myself.
Tell me that they were smart and begged you to attend their school.

Addie: They offered me a place in the program starting this summer…and a scholarship!

Shane: OMG! Yay!!! I'm so proud of you, Adeline.
But with your test scores they would have been idiots not to gobble you right up, you little genius.
I can't wait to say I knew you back before you became a famous architect.

Mitch: Congrats, girl! Though I am a little bummed that you and Nate are moving to New Jersey. Even if it is just for a few years.

Addie: We'll be back to visit all the time. You'll

hardly know we're gone.
But don't tell Nate I got in, okay? I want that to
be a surprise, too.

Mitch: Knowing him, he'll be more excited about
that than the BDSM lingerie.
He's such a nerd. I can't believe I didn't know
what a nerd he was until you two started dating.

Addie: LOL. He hides it well, under all the sexy.

Shane: So do you, sexy thing. Try not to give that
man a heart attack tonight, okay? Take it easy
with the whips and chains until he recovers from
the sight of his true love in bondage gear.

Addie: I AM NOT WEARING BONDAGE
GEAR!
Omg. You two are the worst.
Next time I'm making secret plans with Cat and
Aidan.

Shane: Probably a good idea. I'm still half
convinced that Cat used to be a spy, and Aidan
has the BEST poker face. But for now, you're
stuck with us, sweets.
But don't worry! We won't let you down.

Mitch: No, we won't.
And here's hoping that I WON'T be seeing you
this weekend.

May we both be held captive as willing love slaves until the drive home Monday morning.

Addie: *wine glass emoji* I'll drink to that.

Chapter
TWENTY-FIVE

Nate

"Pull over here." I point to the turn-off before the Lover's Leap Catskill Cabins, the one that leads to the lake, which I was assured by the management is frozen solid and ready for romance.

"She's going to kill me," Mitch moans as he guides Eduardo's BMW over into the gravel. "She swore me to secrecy, and she's so proud of herself for planning this big surprise. It has layers, man. And the first layer was getting you to the cabin without knowing she was there waiting for you."

"Addie goes with the flow. She'll be just as happy to be the surprise-ee as the surprise-er," I say, past ready to see Adeline's face when she sees what I've cooked up. "And when we're done with my surprise, then we can enjoy *her* surprise."

"No, seriously," Mitch says. "She saved her tips from the salon for months so she could pay in cash and you wouldn't accidentally see the room charge on the credit card. She's going to skin me alive."

"And she might not exactly be dressed for the weather," Eduardo says beneath his breath, before adding in a chipper voice. "But that's all right, because I brought her a friend-i-versary present that will keep her toasty and warm."

"I'm sure she'll love whatever it is," I say, touched that Ed got Addie a friend-i-versary present, and so grateful that Ed and Mitch love my girl almost as much as I do. Addie was alone for too long. I love seeing her surrounded by friends and back to being the confidant, take-no-prisoners person I used to know.

"Unless she has a thing against fur." Mitch, always willing to play the Devil's Advocate, pipes up in an ominous tone. "Some people do."

"But it's vintage fur!" Eduardo turns to reach a hand over the front seat, a panicked expression flickering across his face. "Oh my God, Nathaniel, she doesn't have issues with *vintage* fur, does she? I didn't think about that, but it's *vintage*. The poor animals were dead before Adeline was even born, and it's a stunning piece. It was my mother's, and it's such a dainty size. I don't know anyone except Addie who's petite enough to wear it, and I wanted to give her something as lovely as she is. The first friend-i-versary is so important. It really sets the tone, you know…"

"She has no issues with vintage fur that I know of," I say. "Though to be honest, we haven't discussed fur. We're more books, haunted New York, and 'where can we get good tapas after midnight' kind of people."

"Well, I'll just have to hope for the best." Eduardo sighs, pointing at the floorboard by my feet. "Don't forget your basket, Mr. Romance."

"Thanks." I grab my basket, clap Mitch and Ed each on the shoulder and slip out of the backseat with a last, "wish me luck."

"Good luck," Mitch says, while Eduardo calls out in a musical voice, "She's going to say yes, I know it!"

Cursing beneath my breath, I turn to flip the BMW the bird as Mitch pulls away. "Thanks for the jinx, asshole!" I told both of them that this was a "so proud of you for going back to school" surprise, but Eduardo sees all and knows all.

"Don't worry! You can't jinx love," he says with a laugh, waving a hand out the window as the BMW swings into the resort, leaving me alone on the rapidly darkening road. It's just after six, but the winter sun slid behind the mountains nearly an hour ago, which means I'll have to hurry to get everything set up before Ed and Mitch send Addie on her scavenger hunt.

Hitching my basket over my arm, I make my way through the trees to where pines stretch toward the pink and grey sky, casting purple shadows on the frozen lake below. It's as stunning as the pictures on the website, and made even more stunning by the surprise already sitting on the ice near the beach, as promised.

The motorized ice gondola is on loan from Tomahawk Mountain house, delivered this morning because Addie was sad that she didn't get a chance to ride in one last year after the blizzard shut down activity on the lake. I have a slightly shameful amount of money lying around, and I wanted to do something so special that she'll never forget the way I proposed.

Besides, I never would have finished the book that sold my horror trilogy at auction—with movie rights—if Addie hadn't kept pestering me for more pages, giving me the confidence that a love story with a horror garnish was entertaining, if not necessarily marketable. But it turned out that a lot of people thought they could market it, and now Addie and I have the money to move to New Jersey, where I'll write while she goes to school. Mitch refused to tell me if she was accepted to the architecture program at Rutgers, but I have no doubt that she got in. And if she didn't get that scholarship she was gunning for, I have enough to pay her tuition.

And I will pay it, no matter how many times she insists she wants to pay her own way. After the basics are covered—food, shelter, and money for books that aren't carried by the library—money isn't all it's cracked up to be. Hording gold like a dragon who can only nap on a pile of jewels, or scheming new ways to get more when I already have more than enough isn't my jam. I'd rather use my money as a tool to spread happiness, and multiplying Addie's happiness is at the top of my list of things I want to do with my life.

She desperately wants to go back to school, and I desperately want to make all her dreams come true, and so we're going to make it happen.

Together. No matter what.

"Assuming Eduardo hasn't jinxed your ass," I mumble as I spread the blankets I brought out onto the leather seat of the gondola, get the hot chocolate thermos and champagne glasses set up—an engagement calls for something classier than mugs—and hide the big surprise under the driver's seat.

I check that there's enough room to kneel between the seat and the front of the boat, double check that I can reach the ring without sticking my face in Addie's lap—though I will happily bury my face between her sweet thighs as soon as she says "yes"—and then fire up the boat and take it for a test drive.

I'm finishing my first circle around the ice near the shore when I spy a flashlight beam bobbing through the trees between the lake and the resort.

It's her, and it's time.

I flick a switch on the steering wheel, illuminating the tiny lights that cover the gondola and the larger lantern that hangs over the seat from a hook at the rear of the boat. Soft gold beams cut through the deepening purple shadows, warm and welcoming, and then Addie steps out onto the pebble beach and beauty becomes magic.

Chapter
TWENTY-SIX

Nate

She's wearing a dark brown fur coat—Eduardo's gift, I assume—the same shade as the curls floating around her pretty face, that red lipstick that always drives me crazy, and a delighted expression that makes it clear she's perfectly happy to be on the receiving end of the surprise.

Our eyes meet across the ice as I close the distance between us, and her smile widens. "You are one sneaky devil, Nathaniel Casey."

"And you are beautiful, Einstein." I pull the boat to a stop and hop out onto the ice to offer my hand. "May I have the pleasure of ferrying your lovely self around the lake this evening?"

"You may." She inclines her head as she gracefully reaches her gloved hand out to take mine. "Thank you, sir."

"You're very regal and sexy in this fur," I say, helping her into the boat. "I'm not sure I'm fancy enough to sit beside you."

She settles onto the seat, her button nose lifted into the air. "I feel like a Russian princess, I'm not going to lie. We may have to move to Antarctica so I can wear my new precious all year round."

I smile down at her. "So I assume you have no issues with vintage fur?"

"Heck no. It is my precious, and I will call it precious, and it shall be the most precious, for always and forever." She snuggles deeper into the coat with a grin so cute I can't resist leaning down to steal a kiss.

Our lips meet, and I taste sweet and sour and a hint of something that burns my skin. I deepen the kiss, stroking my tongue against hers, amazed that even a year into this constant togetherness thing, a kiss or two is still enough to get me rock-hard and ready.

By the time I take the seat beside her, murmuring "spiked cider," against her lips, I'm already desperate to be inside her.

But my cock has learned the value of delayed satisfaction, and there won't be any naughtiness in the gondola until I have Addie's answer. I want her mind clear when she agrees to marry me, which is why I deliberately chose not to spike the hot chocolate. Her tolerance is a little higher than when we first moved in together, when she would get giggly over the first celebratory glass of champagne and fall fast asleep about halfway through the second, but she's still the lightest of lightweights.

And she's apparently already had something to drink…

"Just a sip," she says, putting my mind at ease. "Eduardo had a thermos and insisted we toast our first friend-i-versary. Isn't that the sweetest thing?"

"It is," I agree, settling beside her and shifting the boat back into drive.

"Not to mention the precious, which I told him was way too much and made the poetry book I bought him seem sad. But he insisted I had to take it, and it's rude to refuse a gift. And you know I hate to be rude."

"I do know this about you." I wrap my arm around her as we cruise away from the Lover's Leap beach, into the deepening shadows beneath the trees and the isolated side of the lake where I intend to make my move. "And I know that I love you a ridiculous amount."

She snuggles closer, making me melt despite the chill in the air. "Me, too. Completely ridiculous, even though you shoplifted my surprise."

"I didn't shoplift it, I added to it." I kiss her forehead, continuing in a softer voice, "So, are you going to keep me in suspense or what?"

"About my surprise?" She nods. "Yes. You

don't get a single hint until after your surprise is over. I want to draw out the surprise fun for as long as possible."

"Sounds good." I turn the wheel, sending our iceboat cruising closer to the center of the lake to avoid a few low hanging tree limbs. "But I meant about Rutgers. We don't have to talk about it tonight if you'd rather not, but I want you to know that I crunched numbers yesterday. We can afford this, Einstein, even if you didn't get the scholarship. It's entirely doable, and I'm not going to stop pestering you about it until you let me help out if you need it."

"That's sweet," she says softly. "But you're assuming that I got accepted."

"What?" I ask, my blood heating. "What the hell is wrong with those people? They should be down on their knees begging you to go to their fucking, piece of shit school. Fuck them! You'll apply somewhere else, somewhere better, where they'll have the sense to—"

"Relax." She laughs as she pats my leg with her gloved hand. "I was just messing with you. I was accepted, I got the scholarship, and I can enter the program in the summer semester, as long as you think we can get moved by then."

Relief floods in to calm my spiking heartbeat. "Of course we can. And shit, that's amazing news! I knew you could do it."

"Thanks." She grins against my lips as she accepts my congratulatory kiss. "And thanks for crunching the numbers, just in case. You are the sweetest and the best."

"And you're a little jerk. You almost gave me a rage-stroke."

She smiles, unrepentantly. "That was revenge for sneaking around and figuring out my surprise. Now we're even." She shakes her head, her brow furrowing. "How did you do it, anyway? I was so careful."

"The lodge called a couple of weeks ago to offer to upgrade us to a hot tub room for free if we added Valentine's Day breakfast reservations," I say, laughing as she curses. "I accepted, of course. Is the hot tub nice?"

"It's very nice, dammit." She wrinkles her nose. "I knew I shouldn't have given them both phone numbers, but I told them to call the cell. Twice! I told them twice, just to be sure they heard me the first time."

"People rarely follow directions."

"Don't I know it," she says with a sigh. "Oh well, that works out well sometimes. If people weren't so bad at following directions, I would still be washing hair instead of managing the Chelsea salon." She glances up at me, worry in her eyes. "I think Eduardo is sad that I'm going to have to quit, even though he promised he was thrilled that I got into the program. I feel terrible for abandoning him."

"He is thrilled for you, don't doubt it for a second. And you'll train a wonderful replacement between now and May, and everything will be fine."

She grins. "Those are some of my favorite words. Everything will be fine."

"Good. Because it will."

Her grin softens as she gazes out across the frozen water. "I believe that now. It really feels like everything is going to be fine. So much better than fine." She threads her fingers through mine. "I love you, P.D. Thank you for this beautiful surprise and this perfect night and for loving me the way you do. You are very good at it—the way that you are very good at all the other things you put your heart into."

We're not to the far side of the lake yet—we're closer to the middle, still in sight of the hotel beach if anyone decides to take an after-dinner walk—but I'm not going to get a better opening than this.

"You're so welcome. It's truly my pleasure." My pulse spikes all over again as I shut off the engine, leaving the lights on because I need to see her face. "But my heart isn't in as deep as I would like for it to be just yet."

Her brow furrows. "It's not?"

I shake my head as I ease off my seat to kneel next to her feet. "No, it's not."

"Oh my God," she murmurs softly, shock and understanding warring in her expression as I reach for the ring hidden beneath the seat. "Oh my God. You're not doing what I think you're doing, are you?"

"That depends." I open the box, revealing the ring my mother brought up last weekend. It's my grandmother's ring, a pink diamond the same color as Addie's cheeks when she blushes. "Are you thinking I'm going to ask you to marry me?"

Her hands fly to cover her mouth, but she nods fast enough to make me think she's eager for me to continue.

"Then yes, I am." I swallow hard, fucking nervous as hell even though I'm pretty sure she's going to say yes. But that doesn't mean I want to half-ass this. I want it to be perfect, as perfect as this woman who has made my life something so much deeper and better and fuller than it was before.

"Adeline Klein," I continue, holding the ring between us, "I knew the moment I laid eyes on you that you were no ordinary girl. And by the time we found our way out of that hellmouth, I was pretty certain kissing you was going to be my goal for the summer. What I *didn't* know back then was that you were the smartest, sweetest, sexiest, most beautiful and perfectly crazy person I would ever meet, or that I would fall so hard for you that no one else ever would, ever could take your place. No one could even come close."

She blinks faster, tears filling her eyes as she tucks her chin to her chest, her mouth still covered by her gloved hands.

"A year ago, fate worked some pretty big

miracles to bring you back to me." I pull the ring free and tuck the box into my coat pocket. "But I still need one more. Because I'm greedy for miracles when it comes to you."

Addie huffs softly with laughter, and sniffs as she pulls her hands from her face, revealing lips pressed into a thin line.

"I need you to say that you'll be my wife, Ad," I say, throat tight. "And promise that we'll spend the rest of our lives making love and making memories and making up for lost time because you are the only person in the world I want to keep growing up with. I want to wake up with you every morning and plan adventures with you every night and be your family, because loving you is the best job on earth, and I don't ever want to quit."

Her eyes close, sending tears down her cheeks. "Oh, man." She sniffs hard again, and dabs gloved fingers beneath her eyes. "The one night I wear mascara, and I can't remember if it's waterproof."

"It doesn't matter. You're beautiful even with black all over your face." I squeeze her knee through the fur of her coat. "But I would love to know your answer. Unless you need time to think…?" She nods, and a piece of my heart breaks off and plummets into my stomach. "Oh. Okay. Yeah, time to think is good. Time to think is probably—"

"No!" She shakes her head just as

emphatically. "No."

"No, you don't want to marry me?" I ask, wondering how this could have gone so differently than I thought it would.

She laughs and shakes her head again. "No, I mean, I don't need time to think. Yes. Yes, I'll marry you. Yes!"

My breath rushes out, and my bones feel less solid than they did a second ago. "Thank God. Shit, you scared me."

"I'm sorry." She leans in, kissing my cheek and then my other cheek and then my lips, long and soft and deep until she's made it abundantly clear how much she meant that "yes."

"You just surprised me is all," she continues, pulling away with a smile. "A proposal wasn't anywhere on my radar. We've only been dating a year, and you've got so much going on with work right now."

"Work schmerk. It'll all get done," I say, but then I start to worry, "But is it soon for you? Would you rather put it off until after you start school? Or finish school? Or—"

"No! Not at all! I can't wait to be your wife." She shakes her head hard enough to send her curls swirling around her face. "I want to keep growing up with you, too. You are my very best friend and the only man I've ever loved and I can't imagine a future without you in it."

"Then do I get to put this on?" I hold up the ring, letting the diamond catch the light of the lantern overhead.

Addie's fingers come to circle my wrist. "Yes, but I do have one serious question. Something important that we should discuss first."

"Shoot." My tongue sweeps out to dampen my lips. I'm starting to wish I'd had a shot before starting this proposal. I seriously underestimated how stressful this would be.

But then Addie has never been the easiest woman to figure out, just the best.

"What about kids?" she asks, proving there's a topic aside from vintage fur that we haven't touched base on. "Do you know if you want kids someday?"

"I want whatever you want," I say, because it's the truth. "I like the idea of babies with you, because I think you'd be a wonderful mom and kids are fun. But after what you went through the first time we got pregnant, I understand if that's not part of your dream for the future. As long as I have you, I'm never going to feel like I'm missing out."

Her eyes start to shine again. "Me, either. As long as I have you. But I would love to have your babies someday, if I can. But before we make any big promises, you should know that I might not be able to." Her brows furrow. "I talked to my doctor after my check-up last fall. She said there's a chance my first pregnancy ended badly because I was so young. But there's a chance that the next time will be hard, too. Maybe even impossible."

"Then we'll adopt."

"Are you sure?" Her frown deepens. "Totally sure?"

"Yes, Addie. I don't need to have my DNA passed down to the next generation."

"But you have very smart, handsome, creative DNA. Wouldn't you be sad not to have a shot at a boy with your cheekbones and way with words, and my really bad hair?"

"I love your hair." I reach out, tugging a curl that bounces immediately back into the halo around her face. "A kid would be lucky to get any part of you, inside or out."

"The hair is better than it used to be, before Eduardo got his hands on it." She smiles, but it doesn't stick around for long. "All joking aside, is that something you're going to regret? If a baby that's a mix of me and you isn't in the cards?"

"Not even a little bit. That's never been what I've thought about when I think about kids."

"Then what do you think about?" she asks, looking intrigued.

I chew on my bottom lip. "Um, well, just…loving them, I guess. Loving them with you, because everything's better with you. And making them happy, and making sure they always know that Mom and Dad are there for them, no matter what. No matter who they want to be, or what they want to dream, or how many mistakes they make on the way to where they're going."

"Yes." She cups my face in her hands. "That's

one of the most beautiful things you've ever said. And you say a lot of beautiful things. I feel the same way. I just want a house where love wins. Where it always wins, even when things get hard."

"It will, I promise," I say, my breath rushing out as I smile. "Now, do I get to put this ring on your finger, Einstein?"

"Yes, pretty devil." Her eyes dance as she holds out her hand. "Please."

Chapter
TWENTY-SEVEN

Nate

I slide the ring down her finger and take a moment to soak it all in, admiring how right it looks there. "That's pretty damned sexy, even if it did used to be my grandmother's."

She laughs. "It is. Which reminds me…" Her eyebrows wiggle up and down as she reaches for the top of her coat and slips the first button free. "My surprise isn't nearly as exciting as yours, but hopefully you'll still be able to enjoy it a little bit."

"I'm sure I'll enjoy it a lot more than a little bit." I watch with undisguised fascination as her fingers work. "Especially if it involves you wearing something sexy under that coat."

"It does, actually." She stands, holding my gaze as she parts the fur, revealing a black leather corset, lace, bows, and a garter belt attached to silky black stockings.

"Fuck," I say, the sight of her stealing all my pretty words away.

She grins. "It's based on a Victorian pattern, like the one Eleanor wears in your book. I thought, what better way to celebrate your book deal than with some historically accurate lingerie?"

"Oh, yes, please." I lean in, running my hands up the backs of her legs beneath the coat, teasing the place where silky stockings becomes silkier skin. "As soon as we get back to the room, I'm taking this off of you with my teeth."

She shivers. "You might need your hands. It's pretty tricky."

"I think you've forgotten how good I am with my mouth."

"Oh no, I haven't." Her lids droop to half-mast as my fingers reach the lace of her panties. "I was thinking about how good you were with your mouth the entire time I was lacing myself in. At one point, I was thinking about it so much that I was tempted to, um…take the edge off before you got here."

I gasp in false horror. "No! You didn't."

"I didn't." She laughs, and then shivers again. "But we have been apart three whole nights. I'm starting to suffer from orgasm deprivation."

My jaw clenches. "I would take care of that right fucking now, but you're already shivering. Sad as it's going to make me, we're going to cover all this back up until we get inside."

"No, it's okay." Her teeth dig into her bottom lip. "It's not that cold. I'll be okay for a little while."

I shake my head. "No way. I'm not risking you getting hypothermia, not after last year. We're going to have responsible fun outside with our clothes on, and then I'll take you inside…" I grip her hips. "Get you out of this coat…" I press a kiss to the soft leather above her belly. "And make you come until you beg me to stop."

Her fingers thread into my hair. "But what if I told you that there are two snaps on the front of my panties," she murmurs as I kiss her again. "That all it would take is a little flick of your fingers and you could have your mouth on me?"

Blood rushing faster, I pull back and look down, immediately finding those two sinful snaps. "You play dirty, Adeline."

"Or you could be inside me," she continues in a soft, sexy voice. "You could unbutton your pants, take out that cock that I enjoy so very much, and I could wrap my new coat around both of us while—"

Her words end in a gasp and rush of laughter as I grab her by the waist and quickly reverse our position. Ten seconds later, I'm on the bench with my cock out in the cold air, Addie's panties have been converted to the crotchless variety, and I'm pulling her back into my arms as she straddles me.

"Inside me," she says in between kisses. "Yes!

I've always wanted to make love to you in an ice gondola."

"Always?" I tease as I slide my fingers through where she's wet and ready.

"Well, since twenty minutes ago when I saw you in an ice gondola." She moans against my lips as I fit the head of my cock to her entrance. "Oh yes, just like that. Oh, God, yes, Nate." Her head falls back as I guide her hips down, down, until I'm buried to the hilt inside my future wife.

"You feel fucking incredible." I grind against her as she begins to move, sliding up and down my shaft. "I can't believe this beautiful, sexy as hell pussy is going to be mine for the rest of my life."

"Yours and only yours." She wraps her arms tighter around my neck, letting her forehead rest against mine. "I love you so much. I can't wait to be Mrs. Casey."

"Because Klein means 'small one'?"

She hums her laugh. "No, though I always felt that was a little on the nose considering no one in my family is over five-four."

"Then why, baby?" My breath catches as she swivels her hips, sending the head of my cock on a blissed-out joyride. "Oh, fuck, that feels good."

"Because then we'll really be a family," she says. "I've missed having a family."

"You're already my family, beautiful. We'll just make it official. God, I love you so much. I love you, Addie Casey."

"Yes. Tomorrow!" She rides me faster, making it hard to focus on anything except how amazing her pussy feels around my cock. "Marry me tomorrow, in this gondola. We'll make Mitch and Ed witness and go home with the same name."

"Yes." I thrust into her welcoming heat as I reach between us, finding her clit below the open panel of the lace. "Let's get fucking married tomorrow."

"Yes, yes." Her breath comes faster as her fingers dig into my shoulders through my coat. "Oh God, Nate, I'm coming. I'm coming so hard."

I groan, moving past words as her body grips my cock, sending me over the edge right after her. I cling tight to Addie, and she clings even tighter to me as we ride out a release so intense it's like an earthquake rocking through my bones.

I actually hear a crackling, crunching sound and hope I haven't broken something vital on the hard wood beneath my ass or thanks to the weird position Addie and I end up in by the time we're finished—half sprawled over the seat and the back of the boat.

But even if it is, she's worth a cracked tailbone or a slipped disc. I will never regret fucking her in the middle of a frozen lake, with my ring on her finger and her dressed to destroy in leather, lace, and fur. I know I'm never going to forget a moment of this night even before Addie says, "Nate, do you see that?"

"See what, babe?" I let my hands skim up and down her thighs, relishing the sensation of still being joined with her as my cock begins to soften.

"See that." She points to the lake as the crackling sound comes again and the line in the ice she's brought to my attention grows a few inches longer.

"Shit." I quickly but carefully pull her from my lap, guiding her to the seat beside me. "Try not to move. I'll get us back to shallow water as fast as I can."

"Jesus," she says, her voice rising as I reach for the wheel. "Is the lake not completely frozen?"

"They told me it was frozen." I turn the key in the wrong direction, then quickly turn it back in the right one, but the only response from the gondola is a clicking sound and a low, unhealthy hum.

"Oh no," Addie says, her words underscored by another sharp crack from the ice beneath us. "Oh God, Nate, this thing won't float, will it?"

"Doubtful considering it's heavy as shit." I turn the key again and again with even more lackluster results. "We may have to make a run for it, Ad, across the ice."

"I'm in high heeled boots." She grabs a handful of my coat and squeezes tight. "But if you hold my hand, I should be okay. Maybe. If we both don't fall through the ice and die. I love you. Just in case."

"I love you, too, but we're not going to fall through the—" I'm cut off by an epic *snap-pop* from the ice and a sharp dip from the front of our gondola as the nose slides down into the lake beneath the too-thin-to-be-safe surface.

I'm bracing myself for the shock of freezing cold water, silently promising myself that I'll get Addie out first and then drag my own sorry ass onto the ice if I have enough strength leftover, when two things happen at once. The lights go out, plunging us into near darkness, save for the halo of the moon rising above the pines. And the gondola jerks sharply backward as if a giant has reached down and pulled us—boat and all—away from the edge.

But the boat doesn't stop when we're back on solid ice.

The gondola keeps sliding steadily backward with a soft *shush shush shush* as it's propelled across the lake by some unseen force, until the lanterns that have flickered on at the hotel beach grow closer and closer.

"What's happening?" Addie whispers, her eyes like saucers in her pale face.

"I don't know," I whisper back. "I'm not driving. The engine isn't even on."

"I can see that." She glances carefully from side to side. "Maybe…magnets?"

"Magnets?" I hiss back. "What kind of magnets?"

"Large magnets that can magically pull boats

out of the water?" Her tone makes it clear she isn't buying her own words. "Or, um…"

Before she can come up with her next theory, we slide across the last few feet of ice and up onto the pebble beach, the wheels of the gondola grinding deep into the gravel beneath. Not one to look an invisible gift horse in the mouth, I jump from the boat and haul Addie out after me.

As soon as I've set her safely on the beach, I grab the blankets, basket, glasses, and thermos, which I pass over to Addie. "No alcohol in there, but it might warm you up, take some of the shock off."

"Thanks," she murmurs in a dazed voice as she reaches for the lid. But before she gets it off, she stops, eyes going even wider as she points to the ice. "Nate, look. On either side of the gondola. Do you see them?"

"See wh…" I trail off as I discover what she's pointing at this time.

Footprints.

There are footprints on either side of the boat, a larger pair on the right and a smaller pair on the left, each print clear in the snow dusted atop the ice. The steps follow the path of the boat right up to the beach, then they turn back, continuing side by side across the lake before disappearing into the forest.

"This place isn't haunted," Addie whispers. "It isn't. I checked. Mitch checked, too, just in case."

"Maybe it isn't the place…"

"You mean, maybe it's us?" she squeaks, swallowing hard. "Oh God, I guess that would make a crazy sort of sense. Well, at least the ghosts were friendly this time, so…that's good?"

"Let's never go out into the woods again. At least, not alone."

"Done." She grabs a handful of my coat as she backs away. "Done and done. In fact, let's go back to the resort right now and find a lot of people to tell all about our engagement and be not alone the rest of the evening."

"Sounds like an excellent plan." I glance her way. "But you should probably button your coat first."

"Right. And you should zip your pants," she says, giggling as I hurry to make myself decent.

As we start up the path a few seconds later, I shout, "Thank you for your help!" into the woods on the other side of the lake, and then Addie and I turn and run. We dash through the trees, across the parking lot, and into the main lodge area where the people at the bar and the restaurant beyond are all too happy to help us toast our engagement. We finish off two glasses of champagne each, and no one says anything about the fact that Addie never takes off her coat.

When the chill is out of our bones, I have a long talk with the manager about their not-nearly-frozen-enough lake, and she promises to give the activities director who approved my gondola plan an earful tomorrow, comp our stay, and help us arrange a quick and lovely marriage ceremony for tomorrow night in the hothouse behind the closed pool.

Addie thanks her profusely, and I do, too, but neither of us says a word about the footprints or the fact that the gondola was dead when it rolled up onto the beach.

After hot chocolate under the stars on our porch, we head inside our cabin and make love again, slower this time, and it's beautiful and real the way it always is. And as we're lying together afterward, watching the fire in the fireplace burn down and arguing about how early is too early to wake Mitch and Eduardo and tell them we're getting married, I decide I wouldn't mind lingering for a little while after death, so long as I get to haunt someplace special with Addie.

"I bet you'd be a hot ghost," I say, fingers trailing up and down her arm.

She hugs me closer. "You, too. I'd help save stupid humans with you."

"Me, too. Stupid humans need all the help we can get."

She presses a kiss to my chest. "I'm just so glad I'm still here with you now."

"Ditto, baby."

She yawns as she curls onto her side, becoming the perfect smaller spoon to my larger one. "Good night, pretty devil. Enjoy your last sleep as a single man."

"I will, " I promise.

And I do, but not as much as I enjoy my first sleep as a married man, and all the nights thereafter.

THE END

Keep reading for a sneak peek of
MASQUERADE WITH THE MASTER
a naughty novella out now!

Sneak Peek
Of
MASQUERADE WITH THE MASTER
A red hot, standalone, super sexy novella…

"Leave the mask on, princess, but everything else comes off. I'm ready to see what's mine."

They say you don't know what you've got until it's gone, but I knew long before the day I said goodbye to Ivy Prescott that I was never going to find another woman like her.

Now, we're both six years older, and my sweet, innocent Ivy has become a sexy, irresistible woman.

She wasn't ready for me then, but she's ready for me now. Ready to learn all the wicked, wonderful things I have to teach her.

Her lesson will begin with a box. A box with a beautiful dress, a mask, and an invitation to come play with a man who has been watching her from afar…

A man who wants to master her—body and soul…

Warning: This sinfully sexy read features

voyeurism, bondage, and a Dominant alpha male who likes to play rough with his toys—but don't worry, he'll make sure you enjoy every scorchingly hot minute of it.

CHAPTER
One

Dear Ivy,

Are you sitting down? If you're not, I advise that you do so.

Put your feet up and get comfortable, doll. This isn't the kind of letter you want to read standing up. Yes, I'm serious. Find a seat for that fine ass of yours and take it.

Now.

There. That wasn't so bad, was it?

Maybe you even liked it. At least a little. Maybe you're intrigued. Eager to learn who has the balls to write a savvy corporate woman like you a letter like this.

I have the balls because I know you,

princess. You like a man who isn't afraid to take control. You always have, even back when you were so naïve that I'm pretty sure you had no idea what I meant when I said I needed to win a woman's submission.

But you got on your knees anyway and asked me to take you to the ball.

Do you remember?

I do. I think about that night—and what a shit job I did of breaking things off—more often than I would like to admit.

But saying good-bye was for the best. I wouldn't have been good for you in the long run. Not back then. I wouldn't have been able to stop myself from taking advantage of your inexperience, no matter how hard I would have tried. We were spark and tinder, Prescott, and I would have burned you to the ground.

But things are different now...

Aren't they?

I know how you spend your Saturdays, Ivy. I know about the secret staircase, the red door, and the toys you play with in the back room with a man who wants you to call him Master. But you weren't meant for him.

You were meant for me.

If you're shaking your head—or having a hard time coming to grips with this blast from the past—ask yourself this: Whose face do you see when you close your eyes and slip your fingers between your legs? Whose hands are brushing across your nipples, smoothing over your ass, spreading your thighs wide? Whose voice is in your ear, telling you how sweet you taste, how perfectly wet you are, how much he wants to fuck you and keep fucking you until there is no doubt in your mind who your pleasure belongs to?

Tell the truth, princess. Don't lie to me, or to yourself.

Maybe you're even turned on right now. Wet. Thinking about how good we were together and all the fun we could have now that your kink has caught up with mine.

I hope so. Because I want to be with

you, Ivy—in person, unfiltered, no holds barred and no holding back. I want to push your skirt up around your hips and get my mouth between your legs. I want to tie your wrists to my headboard and tease you until you beg me to take you. I want to make love to you in every filthy way you've daydreamed about and a few new ways I'll teach you because I'm a dirty bastard with a filthy mind and you are the star of every single one of my fantasies.

I want to pleasure you, possess you. I want it so bad I can almost taste the salt and honey of your skin.

No one tastes like you. So sinfully sweet...

I've been thinking so often lately about that camping trip on the beach, of that first kiss mixed with rain and the way you came on my mouth with the wind howling outside our tent. You were lightning in a bottle, and I knew that first night that I was never going to find another woman like you.

Which brings us to this moment.

This gift, and a chance to see if lightning can strike twice.

In the letter I sent with that first tuition check, I warned that there would come a day when your "anonymous friend" would ask for a favor. I also said that you would be free to say yes or no to that request—no hard feelings; no harm, no foul. I meant it then, and I mean it now. There is no debt to be repaid, only an opportunity sincerely offered.

I want to show you all the things I've learned since the night we parted ways. I want to show you how sorry I am, and how truly incredible submission can feel. That man you've dabbled with doesn't have what it takes to top you, but I do. Meet me tonight and let me prove it.

You're ready for the ball, princess, and I would so very much like to be the man to take you.

I'll send a car at eight.

Sincerely,
Edward

Masquerade with THE MASTER

is available now!

Acknowledgements

Thank you to everyone who has fallen in love with the crew at Magnificent Bastard Consulting and dropped a line telling me to write faster. Knowing I've made you smile, laugh out loud, and occasionally snort a beverage through your nose onto your e-reader is pretty much the best thing ever. I truly love writing these books so much, and truly appreciate all of you.

I'm sad to see these characters go, but I'm SUPER excited about my next romantic comedy series. I can't wait for you to meet the red hot, hysterical men of the Oregon Bad Motherpuckers hockey team in HOT AS PUCK out in April.

Xo,
Lili

Tell Lili your favorite part!

I love reading your thoughts about the books and your review matters. Reviews help readers find new-to-them authors to enjoy. So if you could take a moment to leave a review letting me know your favorite part of the story—nothing fancy required, even a sentence or two would be wonderful—I would be deeply grateful.

About the Author

Lili Valente has slept under the stars in Greece, eaten dinner at midnight with French men who couldn't be trusted to keep their mouths on their food, and walked alone through Munich's red light district after dark and lived to tell the tale.

These days you can find her writing in a tent beside the sea, drinking coconut water and thinking delightfully dirty thoughts.

Lili loves to hear from her readers. You can reach her via email at lili.valente.romance@gmail.com or like her page on Facebook
https://www.facebook.com/AuthorLiliValente

You can also visit her website:
http://www.lilivalente.com/

Also By Lili Valente

Sexy Flirty Dirty Standalone
Romantic Comedy:

Magnificent Bastard
Spectacular Rascal
Incredible You
Meant For You

Master Me Series
(super naughty bedtime stories!):

Snowed in with the Boss
Masquerade with the Master

Under His Command Series:

Controlling Her Pleasure
Commanding Her Trust
Claiming Her Heart

Bought by the Billionaire Series:

Dark Domination
Deep Domination
Desperate Domination
Divine Domination

Kidnapped by the Billionaire Series:

Dirty Twisted Love
Filthy Wicked Love
Crazy Beautiful Love
One More Shameless Night

Bedding the Bad Boy Series:

The Bad Boy's Temptation
The Bad Boy's Seduction
The Bad Boy's Redemption

29894663R00175

Printed in Great Britain
by Amazon